SLAPSHOT
AUSTIN ACES HOCKEY CLUB

TL HAMILTON

AUSTIN ACES HOCKEY

To all the black sheep and ugly ducklings.
Fuck the haters.
You deserve a Happily Ever After

MEET THE AUSTIN ACES

Austin Aces Hockey Club... where sworn enemies become lovers... on and off the ice.

Join eight of your favorite 🏒 romance authors and get in on the action...

One Touch by Linden Rowe
Unleashed by Jenna McCall
Power Play by C.M. Kane
Slapshot by TL Hamilton
Tripped Up by Allie Lasky
On Thin Ice by Rebecca Norinne Caudill
Puck Drop by Andie Bale
Goalie Interference by Kim Findlay

CHAPTER
ONE

Blair

"Come on, Viggy. I know you gave me a smile in there somewhere—There it is. Good."

I paused the footage and took a screenshot of the captain of the Austin Aces hockey team, smirking. Fans would love it.

Backing the footage up a couple of seconds, I isolated the moment and spliced it into a teaser trailer of this season's lineup. Some of the content had been recycled from previous years, while other files were footage I'd filmed during the development camp in July.

"Now, let's see if I can find when Oscar..." I grinned as I clicked into the video of the giant winger striking a flamenco pose and cha-cha-ing in full gear. He'd told me that he and his wife regularly took dance classes together, and the way he said it felt like he was giving me TMI, but I had to admit that he could move both on and off the ice.

Pausing on a closeup of his goofy grin, I took my glasses

off and stretched, wincing as my spine snapped, crackled, and popped—a reminder to move that was more effective than my fitness watch's hourly beep to the tune of *move your ass*. The glow of my laptop was the only source of light in the room, and after God knew how long in front of the computer, my dry eyes were screaming for a break. Huh. Five hours. My stomach rumbled, and I reached for the melted iced latte I'd bought at Starbucks on my way home from the rink.

I really should eat something healthy.

The idea of cooking any of the wilted vegetables I'd bought during a wave of health-related inspiration felt like too much work, so with a half-hearted promise to cook the following night, I opened my browser. A burger with tomato on it was almost the same as eating a salad. Right? As the website thanked me for my order and estimated delivery time at forty minutes, my cell rang.

Fishing through my drink collection—mango boba, 'hot' coffee, iced latte, and a Stanley cup full of untouched, room temperature water—and casting aside yesterday's T-shirt that hadn't made it to the hamper, I groaned as I caught sight of who was reaching out to touch me and seriously considered letting the thing ring out. The problem was that the caller was a level of tenacious that she could choose to turn up on my doorstep in less time than my burger and fries.

I pushed the bulk of my curls away from my ear and prayed for patience as I accepted the call.

"Hey, Mom. How are you?"

"Duckie. I didn't expect you to answer your phone. You can be so difficult to contact."

I cringed at the old nickname and mentally tallied the

first criticism of the phone call. First sentence. She was off to a solid start.

"Well, work keeps me busy. I can't always answer."

"When are you getting a real job? Instead of being an instafluencer, or whatever it is, you should be doing something with that brain of yours. Such a waste, especially when... you know."

I considered reminding her that Social Media Manager for the Austin Aces was a respectable job, especially at twenty-three, but she was already onto her next favorite topic.

"Georgia has a very promising audition coming up next week. She could be on the television soon. She'll be famous. She's grown into such a beautiful woman."

In the space of thirty seconds she had insulted my job, reminded me how superior my sister was to me, and alluded to my unfortunate looks.

Bravo, Mom. New record.

I considered knocking myself out on my desk to avoid the need to engage in the rest of this conversation. Unfortunately, I was chicken shit when it came to pain, so I'd just have to grit and bear it for at least another... The minute hand clicked over on my wall clock. Two minutes before I could beg off and end the conversation.

"...you really should take what you can get, so I told him you were free this Friday."

"What?" I cut in on my mother's insult-riddled monologue.

The long-suffering sigh told me I was a disappointment and a lost cause all rolled up in one difficult-to-accept package.

"The Ronson boy. He always liked you when you were

young. He has an overnight stopover in Austin on Friday night and has agreed to take you out."

An image came to mind of a ten-year-old boy whose hair had been thinning even then. His dark eyes, small and shifty, had always been too close together, and his forefinger on an eternal journey between his nostril and his mouth. He had somehow always smelled of wet dog, despite having had a severe allergy to the species; the musty, earthy, slightly fecal odor a constant mystery to every kid unfortunate enough to be forced into a play date with the guy.

"Not Snot Ronson. Seriously, Mom? I'm not going out with that guy." The clock ticked over another minute, and I watched with rapt attention, wondering if I needed to just bite the bullet and go into hiding. I could change my name and become a circus performer... Except I was scared of heights. And was about as flexible as a loaf of bread. I could bend, but there was a good chance I'd just break in two.

"He's grown up so much since you last saw him."

"Wasn't he arrested last year for stalking?"

"The allegations were unfounded. It was all a misunderstanding. His poor mother had to have a word with that wicked woman... Anyway. Enough of that. You're lucky he's available and willing to spend time with you. You don't want to end up a spinster, stuck at home with her cats."

Aaannnd I was done. Knocking on the underside of my desk, I feigned an approximation of upset.

"I'm so sorry, Mom. Someone's at the door. I'm going to have to go."

"I just want what's best for you, Duckie. I can't stand the idea of having a daughter who ends up alone because she left it too late. You don't have options like your sister does."

"Love you too, Mom. Bye."

Ending the call, I dropped my head onto the desk and winced at the impact. Worth it.

Maybe if I killed enough brain cells, I could forget the conversation and pretend my mother didn't think I was so hideous that I needed to be set up with a nose picking stalker to get laid.

Making a note in my calendar to ensure I would be indisposed on Friday, I turned back to my laptop, determined to finish my work. At least there was one area of my life where I was valued.

My hand knocked against the boba cup and, without shifting my eyes from the computer screen, I lifted the straw to my lips. Peach green tea shot into my mouth in a fresh rush, my body relaxing in sugary contentment as I burst the mango popping balls against the back of my teeth.

As my family-induced poor self-image took a backseat, I refocused on the still of Oscar Cavanaugh aka Caveman. The third line winger was a PR dream. A goofy, good-looking guy who was respectful to everyone and utterly devoted to his wife.

He was good people.

Unwittingly, my eyes shifted to the other person in the still. Dark brown hair cascaded from his head in an artfully styled wave that rested at his collar. That head was tilted back, straight, white teeth visible as he laughed at his friend's antics. Even his freaking laugh lines were beautiful, and despite them being crinkled with mirth, I knew the exact shade of olive green his eyes were when he was in that mood. Mindlessly, I traced the perfectly groomed scruff of beard on his jaw and wondered—not for the first time—if those lips were as soft as they looked.

A knock at my door pulled me from my musings, and as the smell of greasy fries and melted cheese hit my nose, I cursed myself.

He may be beautiful, but Cian O'Leary was an asshole.

I might have had a moment of weakness in the privacy of my own home, but there was no way that I would ever consider him anything more than the self-involved, better-than-everyone type of character that all people blessed with good genetics were.

He'd end up with some supermodel in the near future who could sit with him during their boring, beautiful dinners and trade compliments about their appearance until they went to their beds.

For beauty sleep, naturally.

Those type of people ran the world.

Just ask my sister.

CHAPTER
TWO

Cian

"I<small>T'S</small> *a stunning eighty-nine-degree morning here in Austin, Texas, and you're listening to 105.4 AARX FM. Stay tuned for the latest highlights in the GWL. The San Antonio Rattlers are going head-to-head with The Chicago Engines—"*

Killing the engine, I bounced out of my truck, practically skipped to the property's front door, and let myself in without bothering to knock.

Oscar and his wife, Mia, had moved into this two-bedroom villa in Barton Creek shortly after we were drafted to Austin. Six months later, after I'd tried the transient accommodation provided by the team and found it less than inspiring, I'd rented my own single bedroom place two blocks from them.

"Wakey wakey, time to go, Caveman!" I called, slamming the door hard behind me. While I had no problem inviting myself in, and Oscar and I had lived together for years in college, I'd walked in on them in compromising positions one too many times to risk catching them unaware.

The smoky scent of bacon flavored the air, and I followed my nose to the kitchen to find the man bent over the cooktop.

"I'll be ready in a minute, just making sure Mia eats today."

As he spoke, he dipped a thick cut of bread into an eggy mixture and threw it on a second pan. A rush of cinnamon and butter made my mouth water, and if it hadn't been the first day of training camp, I would have insisted he fry some up for me.

"That smells amazing, but if that's in your gut, I'm not going to envy you in a couple of hours."

"Oh, don't worry. I had granola. Only Mia gets the good stuff today."

"Damn straight." Mia breezed into the room in a cloud of the *Paradox by Prada* perfume that I helped Oscar pick out for her for Valentine's Day. Her long, black hair swept around her hips as she sashayed over to her hubs and pulled him into a kiss. These guys were goals, for real.

I let them have a minute, but when Oscar's hands started wandering, intervention was required to avoid us being late. Snatching a tea towel, I twisted the fabric into a tight curl and snapped it at his ass, enjoying the squeal of surprise almost as much as the glower I received for my efforts.

"You're an asshole."

"And we're going to be late unless you move your ass. Mia, you look gorgeous, as always, but we have to hit the road."

Oscar sighed and slowly disengaged from Mia, dropping a final kiss on her nose before jogging off. He returned a moment later with his kit bag over his shoulder, pausing long enough to pin his wife with a faux-stern look. Mia just rolled her eyes, taking a large bite of toast before she gave him an obnoxious wave.

"And time to go," I announced, grabbing my friend by the shoulder and shoving him out the door before he could get caught up again.

"I love you!" he called as I slammed the door and ushered him toward my truck.

"I think you have her pretty safely locked down now. You can ease up on all the lovey shit, man," I groused, cranking the engine and leaving a cloud of diesel in our wake.

He laughed and patted my head. "Not gonna happen. I know how good I got it with her, and I'm not ashamed to be loud about it. She deserves to spend every day knowing exactly how I feel. You'll get it one day."

I shuddered and knocked his hand away.

"I don't think so. You guys are a once in a lifetime thing. I don't think it's on the cards for me. I'll just have to keep letting bunnies warm my bed until I retire, then it's back home to help with the dogs."

If I thought I'd get some sympathy out of my friend for the bleak forecast on my life, I'd forgotten who I was speaking to.

"First, you would need to actually be in the habit of picking up bunnies to have them warm your bed. And second, I will personally make sure you have a granny flat on my future property before I let you go home permanently. You can be a manny for all our kids, it'll be great."

"Does Mia know about this plan?"

"Nah, but she'll be fine with it."

I huffed, scraping a hand through my hair. She would be, too. Mia had never met my parents, and we never spoke about our upbringing together, but like recognized like when it came to trauma, regardless of the individual experience.

Oscar and I both knew I didn't want to end up back at home. Hell, visiting my parents was hard enough, but I'd keep checking in on them because it was what I did.

I made sure that everyone was okay.

Settling into a comfortable silence, we let the banter of morning radio fill the air as we approached the bridge over the Colorado River.

"I wonder how much they've changed up the lines this year," Oscar muttered as we pulled into the parking lot at the Aces Performance Center. The state-of-the-art building was a labyrinth of hallways branching off into rooms for player development and R&R, as well as staff offices and facilities. In the far reaches of the building, on the second floor, the executives and management sat in well-furnished offices that we all hoped never to visit. In the center of everything was my favorite place in the building. The rink.

As we stepped through the doors, the kiss of chilled air on my skin made me grin in anticipation. I lived for hockey. My earliest memories were of skating around the pond at the back of my parents' property on cold winter mornings, firing pucks into a makeshift goal my dad had put together with branches and an old bedsheet. The skates were too big, my stick was too small, both thrifted from the Goodwill two towns over, but I didn't care about anything once I was out on the ice. Even now, in the heat of a game, I never felt more in control, more free, than when I was speeding over the ice.

"Let's get out there," I said, slapping Oscar on the

shoulder and heading toward the rink to check in before I dumped my gear in the change rooms.

"This is going to be a good year. I can feel it."

"Can you feel it in your flow?" he asked, tugging at my hair. I batted his hand away. "Maybe I can. If that's your way of asking if I'm keeping it this year, you bet your ass I will." I gave him a cheeky wink and hiked my kit bag higher on my shoulder, shaking my hair out behind me.

I'd thought about cutting it, but after getting so close to the finals last year, I didn't want to risk losing the luck. Literally cutting it out, if you will. It was at collar length, and as long as I remembered to brush it, it wasn't too much of a hassle.

Plus, I liked it.

Oscar grunted. For someone with a near-paralyzing fear of birds, he had a remarkable disdain for charms and superstition. He never seemed to complain when the hair came through and gave us the W, though.

A bright laugh echoed around the rink and a flash of bright orange curls flew past half a second before someone in full gear. The number seventy-seven on his back let me know it was Lathan Silver, the team's other alternate captain, getting in early for ice time. As they circled back, I tried and failed to ignore the one sticking point in my otherwise perfect world.

Blair Kennedy was a social media manager who knew her stuff. The marketing campaigns and social posts she coordinated for the team socials, as well as every individual player, were top quality and frequently went viral. I'd heard her talk shop like one of the old pros, and as she took another lap with Silver, I had to admit her skate work was flawless. Her homely looks belied a personality that shone on every person she interacted with... except me.

For some unknown reason, every time I looked into those plain brown eyes, pure hatred radiated back at me. Oscar told me I was exaggerating. I told him there were twenty-five formal fundraising events that had Aces players in attendance the previous year. Only one player had been forced to attend every single one. This guy.

Until the tenth event, I hadn't even owned a tuxedo.

When it became obvious it would be an ongoing thing, I'd quit hiring the damn things and had one tailored.

I still hated wearing it.

"This year's going to be different," I vowed as she broke away from the right winger and headed for the boards, smiling at my friend. As she noticed me standing beside him, the warmth washed out of her features.

"I'm going to make her like me."

THREE

Blair

NEW DAY, *new me.*

My nose and cheeks hummed in the cold air as I finally let Silver off the hook and put down my camera. We had some great action shots for his personal social account, and some that would go straight into the file for promotional use.

The phone call with my mother the night before still hung heavy over my head, but after a couple hours of sleep and two venti lattes from Starbucks on my way in, I was determined to shed the negativity of the night before and focus on what I loved. Hockey.

A shaggy head of dirty blond hair on a ridiculously tall body made me grin. Waving hello, I skated toward Cavanaugh to see how it had gone with the class he told me about the night before... only to realize he wasn't alone.

The silken dark hair on a slightly shorter, though no less built, body shouldn't have been a surprise, but maybe I needed a little more coffee before I dealt with that particular player.

"You're here early," Oscar said as I opened the gate and resolutely avoided his friend's gaze.

"No rest for the wicked," I quipped. "But hopefully, there's more coffee in my future. Are you headed in to get changed? We can do some stills before training starts."

Oscar's eyes were warm as he clapped me gently on the shoulder, but as he opened his mouth, another voice cut in.

"Sounds great." The deep timbre sent an unwelcome shiver of pleasure through my body. Despite his surname and obvious Irish features, his accent was all American and far too pleasant, considering my adamant dislike of the man.

"Actually, I was talking to—"

"I'll just need a minute to kit up, then I'm all yours until Coach wants us."

His olive-green eyes sparkled with a teasing light that I was sure he used to get what he wanted from everyone around him. It was too early to deal with him, but at least I'd have a chance to get another coffee before I hit the ice with him. Then I could avoid him for the rest of the day.

Sacrifice now for peace of mind later.

"Fine. I'll meet you here after I get coffee."

He was already backing toward the change rooms, maintaining eye contact like he thought I'd disappear the second he turned his back. The thought was tempting, and my usual MO when I could get away with it. I tried to create his content with footage recorded during games or, when necessary, filmed in conjunction with Oscar's stuff. The 'Caveman' was a human social lubricant, using his ridiculous good looks and extroverted personality to make any interaction pleasant. Even with certain persons who could remain unnamed.

"Oh, I'd love one, thanks."

The bastard flashed me a blinding smile and winked, jogging off before I could remind him I wasn't his goddamn assistant.

Maybe I'd spit in his coffee. It would serve him right.

No more negativity, remember?

Shit. Okay. I could be civil.

Trading my skates for Crocs—when I was changing shoes all day sneakers weren't practical, and heels were a torture device I reserved for times when I couldn't avoid them—I went across the road to the Wild Brew Cafe where everyone knew my name... because I was in there several times a day.

The rich scent of coffee beans and sugar hit me like a wave as I pushed through the door and I paused for a moment, breathing the scent deep into my lungs and enjoying the somatic reset it offered. Instant calm.

"Usual, Blair?" Toni, the store manager, asked, already reaching for the largest cup they sold.

"Make it two, please." I could be nice. And if it wasn't to his taste, then I could drink it. Win/win.

"How's the team looking this year?" Toni asked over the squeal of the frother wand. The Canadian barista had made the move to Austin twelve months before to meet up with her high school flame after they matched on a dating app. Their story was something straight out of a sapphic novel and I'd even managed to meet her partner a time or two when the need for coffee had brought me out into the Austin heat in search of my caffeine fix. The only thing Toni ever mentioned regretting about the move was the weather, and the American preference for football over hockey.

"The development camp went really well last month. A lot of players to watch in the next few years. Training camp starts today, though, and the vibe is awesome. Everyone's excited to get back on the ice."

The bean grinder interrupted our conversation for a moment and, like an addict, I took a deep breath of the sharp earthy scent.

"Good to hear. Kate bought us both season tickets this year, so we'll be in the stands cheering them on."

Toni didn't miss a beat with the syrup, cream, and toffee chips, handing over the two cups with a wink.

"I'll see you in a couple of hours?"

I laughed and took a test sip, not quite suppressing a moan.

"You know it."

Saluting her with my cup, I returned to the heat of the day and hustled back to the rink to get Cian O'Leary's content over and done with.

"Blair. Do you have a minute?"

Dante appeared out of a corridor on my right, signaling with her head to follow as she continued on without breaking stride. As usual, her blonde hair was perfectly styled in a neat French twist, her power suit screaming boss bitch to the tune of her sensible black pumps clicking across the floor. I looked down at my overalls and Crocs and, once again, felt the inadequacy build. Even when I put effort in, I never looked as cool as her.

"Are you coming?"

Shaking myself out of the impromptu self-flagellation session, I repeated my mantra and fell into step behind her.

New day, new me.

No more picking apart my appearance. No more negativity.

This self-improvement stuff was fucking hard.

Dante strode through the door of one of the vacant offices and turned, resting her hip against the empty desk. She crossed her arms and studied me with a critical eye as I followed her inside.

"Close the door for a sec."

"Okay... Is everything alright? I'm supposed to be getting some shots in with O'Leary before they start for the day."

I stood awkwardly in the space, both hands full of coffee cups and wishing I'd tied my unruly hair back. A ginger curl stuck to my lashes as I blinked. Using my forearm, I tried to brush it away but failed, as my glasses foiled my attempts. With a sigh, I gave up and set the cups down on a low counter, finally giving my full attention to my supervisor.

"This won't take long. How have you been liking your role with the Aces?"

Her face was inscrutable.

Had I done something wrong?

The coffee cups beside me felt like glaring accusations of wasted time and resources. Maybe I should have taken less breaks.

Her pale blue eyes were steady as she waited through my internal panic.

Speak, idiot.

"Uhh, I love it here. It's my dream job, so yeah. I, um... love it."

Heat crawled up my neck and I cursed my pale skin. I never did well with confrontation because it was difficult to keep a position of power while glowing like a traffic light.

"What are your plans for the future?"

Considering she clearly meant further afield than drinking the coffee beside me and surviving the session with O'Leary, I didn't know how to answer her.

"I'm not sure, but I hope it will involve staying with the Aces, or at the very least, working in hockey," I said carefully, studying her perfectly made-up features for hints of what this could be about.

In an uncharacteristic move, she broke eye contact first, taking a stroll around the empty office. The window was her first stop. Cracking the blinds, she gazed outside for a moment, like there might be something interesting in the staff parking lot. Without a word, she let them fall shut and ran her fingers across the desk next, brushing the dust off on her skirt before returning to her lean in front of me.

"This isn't common knowledge yet, but I don't plan to renew my contract with the Aces next year. I love this job and the team, but it's time for something new for me."

I tried but failed to hide my reaction. Everyone knew Dante was one of the best in the business. She had gotten more players out of hot water than I'd had caffeine-free days… Okay, bad analogy. But she was a badass at what she did.

"So… what do you think?"

Her expression was expectant, and I silently cursed my distraction. What had she asked?

"I… don't know…" Was I really in a position to cast judgment on her life choices?

"You're great at what you do, and I feel like with a little training and a lot more self-confidence, you'd be a perfect fit. I could mentor you through this season."

Did she mean…?

"You want me to go for the PR position?"

Dante's brow wrinkled like we were speaking two different languages.

"That's what I said. What do you think?"

A buzzing started at my toes, that flush making a reappearance in my cheeks, causing my scalp to itch. PR manager for the Austin Aces. I'd never considered moving that high because I couldn't imagine the team without Dante at the head of it. But under her mentorship, it could be me next year.

Immediately, negative thoughts streamed in, to the tune of *not good enough, too unsophisticated,* and *who do you think you are?* The voice, I realized, was my mother's.

She could take my self-image, but I'd be damned if she took my professional one. With a deep breath, I mustered a smile for Dante.

"I'd love to."

CHAPTER
FOUR

Cian

BLAIR WAS PRACTICALLY VIBRATING out of her skin when she returned to the rink. Without a fuss, she handed me a huge coffee cup and bent to pull her skates on.

"Thanks. You didn't spit in it, did you?" I joked, taking a sip and almost choking on the sweetness. Okay, if she had the same thing as me, it made sense that her nervous system was about to crash. Sending up a prayer for my blood sugar levels, I took a gulp, not willing to piss her off if this was some kind of olive branch.

"I thought about it, but no. Come on. Let's get this done."

She slid her cell out of her pocket and affixed it to the selfie stick thing she usually used on the ice. Tapping at the screen, she skated toward the center of the ice, completely absorbed in whatever settings she was playing with. Her confidence on skates was something I knew on the same level I knew when to take the shot during a game and when to go for the assist. It was innate. But as I followed her onto the rink, it occurred to me that she was too good for just a regular skater.

I wondered if she had played in the past. Or maybe did another ice sport like figure skating or something. Maybe I could ask her. It was the kind of thing people did when they were making friends.

"Hey, how did you—"

Blair looked up from her phone. "We're going to do an easy lap to start. No helmet, just vibing on the skates."

I nodded, swallowing the question as she returned the gesture and skated backward with her phone trained on me. With the door firmly shut on conversation, I settled into the session and found it was a lot more fun than I'd thought. Blair had no trouble keeping up, even when I pulled an asshole move and started sprinting, just to see what she'd do. It made me think of all those adventurer shows where the host would climb the big dangerous thing and dramatically take all the praise for being fearless when they had a camera crew doing the same exact thing while also making the host look good on camera. That was Blair. A freaking boss. Keeping up while also steadying a camera that would make me look like a star.

By the time Marco Russo, our assistant coach, caught my attention to inform me it was time to start training, I was warm and feeling the good vibes. This was the year. No more bad blood between me and Blair.

"Before you go," she called, catching the gate behind me. I raised a brow and waited. "There's a function Friday night. The Aces need a presence there and you're it."

I groaned, feeling the happiness drain out of me at the thought of formal suits and ego massaging.

"Surely, there's someone else..."

"Nope. You're it, alternate captain. Make sure you get any dry-cleaning that you need done. You have to look your best for the start of season."

I swiped a hand over my face, hoping that when I met her gaze again, I'd see any hint that she was fucking with me. Nope. Her eyes were steady, content to wait for my agreement while I knew damn well I needed to get my ass to the change rooms.

Did I say she was good at her job? Maybe she was just a hardass.

"Who else is going?"

"Just me. It's a smaller event, but you still need to be there."

Only us. What a perfect opportunity to build goodwill.

All of a sudden, I wasn't so annoyed.

"Okay, we'll carpool. Send me the details and I'll pick you up."

"Wait... what?" Her mouth dropped open as I felt the rightness of the decision settle over me.

"Wear something pretty for me." I winked as I took off to join my team.

Fine, maybe the last comment had been a jerk move, but if I changed too much, she'd get suspicious about my new decision for us to be besties. It never sat right when someone disliked me, so I was going to change it. Starting now.

Day one of training was hectic. Coach always made a point of pushing us until one of the rookies hurled. This year, it was almost me after the sugary nightmare I'd consumed earlier. Maybe Blair hadn't spit in it because the drink itself was an act of sabotage.

I sat rink side and peeled my skates off, already thinking

of the showers when the devil herself flopped down beside me.

"Hey, I have a questionnaire for you to fill out, but your email address isn't working. Is it still... sk8godd99 at AOL?"

"Yeah, sorry. I changed it. I'll give you the new one." I rubbed the back of my neck, cringing at the email address I'd kept far too long. We had email addresses through the Aces organization, but I never checked it and had tried to make things easier by providing my personal email in my first year. The email I gave her was a new one I'd made with my first name and last name. Like a normal person. And I was equal parts happy and kind of nervous at the evidence of adulthood. Seemed pretty stupid to think like that when I had a million-dollar contract and had lived out of home since going to college, but it was what it was. Blair's cell rang on the bench beside her, and the look on her face reminded me of how I felt when mine rang sometimes.

"Excuse me," she muttered, turning her back.

"Hey, Mom, I'm at work at the moment..."

"Duckie! I'm just calling to ask about..." Blair glanced at me and grimaced, stalking away before I could hear more of the conversation. Her family called her Duckie? That was adorable. I tucked that information away for safekeeping and headed for the change rooms, pausing at the sound of my name.

Blair had paused, one hand over her phone like she could keep our interaction quiet from her mother on the other end.

"Can you let them know I'll be in in a second? I'll just deal with this quickly."

I gave her a thumbs up as she returned to her call and continued on my way.

My shirt stuck to me under my gear, the sweat drying in

an itchy mess that smelled of salt and musty clothes. My thighs and ass throbbed with a pleasant ache that had been missing from my off-season training. I pushed myself hard, but not first-day-of-training-camp hard. Making a note to buy magnesium at the store on the way home, I found my cubby beside Oscar's and started to strip off my gear.

The noise in the locker room was about what you'd expect from a group of men over-tired and running on adrenaline and endorphins after a day on the ice. Near deafening. Still, over the dull roar, one voice still managed to edge the others out.

Chet Doyle.

The asshole had an opinion on everything and a belief that every person in his vicinity was aching to know what those opinions were.

We didn't.

We really didn't.

His braying laugh cut through the room and, if the flush on the back of Stryker Bell's neck was anything to go by, he'd just said something highly offensive to amuse himself.

The openly bisexual winger was a frequent target of Doyle's 'jokes' and a quick glance at Oscar told me he was ready to throw down for his line mate. Neither of us had time for Chet's bullshit.

"Give it a rest," I drawled before Oscar got any ideas.

"Ah, decided to join us, did you, O'Leary?" Doyle pushed to his feet and strode into the middle of the room like he was ready to hold court or some shit. "Thought you were busy with the hot mess social media bitch."

"You mean the hot mess that's so talented she can make even you look good? Nah, we're finished for now."

I slipped off my jersey and started shedding padding, hoping he'd leave it at that.

"I always look good. Which is more than I can say for her. Why are you sniffing around that, anyway? Thinking of making her your charity fuck for the season?" Someone on the other side of the locker room made an attempt to shut him up, but he had hooked in with a tenacity that was great on the ice, and fucking annoying anywhere else.

"Is it the dog face? Or the red hair? I know they say redheads are great in the sack, but have some dignity, man."

Normally, I would have ignored Chet until he lost interest, but Blair was due to walk through the double doors behind the loudmouth any second, and she didn't need to hear him wasting oxygen about this shit.

"I'm not trying to nail her, okay? Just doing my job."

Doyle's mouth quirked in a nasty way that told me things were about to get worse.

"Is that because you can't? Yeah, that's it. She's turned you down."

"No."

"One hundred bucks says you can't bang her before playoffs."

The locker room was oddly quiet, and I wished someone would do something to take the attention off the train wreck I seemed to be in.

"I'm not making a bet to bang someone. It's juvenile and really fucking disrespectful."

Chet scoffed. "Fucking doesn't need to be disrespectful. Hell, her body seems half decent under all the shitty fashion choices. Put a paper bag over her head and put her on her knees."

"Fuck off, Doyle."

"Seriously. Maybe getting laid will be good for you. Practice on her and build your game for the bunnies." He cocked his head in faux sympathy. "Have you forgotten how it all works?"

My grip tightened on the skates I was returning to their spot in my cubby.

I certainly wasn't considering using them to shut up my teammate. Noooooo. Not at all.

Out in the hall, a feminine laugh echoed far too closely to the locker room doors.

"Leave it. She's just outside."

He held his arms wide, turning to take in the rest of the team as they all sat around with varying degrees of dislike on their faces. "Maybe she deserves to know the truth. That she can't even get laid when there's money on the table." The sneer that lifted his lip turned the asshole into something as ugly as his words. As he spoke, he increased his volume until I was sure Blair could hear every word.

"She should know that the great Cian O'Leary would rather abstain from sex and give me money to—"

The door cracked open.

"Fuck, alright fine. Just shut up."

Satisfied that he'd won this round, Doyle turned toward the doorway.

"Oh, hi Blair," he said with a smug grin.

"Ahhh, hi, Chet. How's it going?" she asked, noting how every set of eyes in the room was trained on her.

"Is everything alright, guys?" As though the room had taken a collective inhale, chatter returned in a rush, and I flopped on the bench in front of my locker, surreptitiously watching Blair for any sign she may have heard the previous discussion.

"That was a bad idea, man," Oscar whispered, whipping a towel around his hips.

"Like I had a choice. I couldn't let her hear that," I grumbled.

The look he gave me warned I may still have chosen the worst of the two options.

I hoped he wasn't right.

FIVE

Blair

"FOR THE LOVE OF GOD, please just..." I added more water to the front section of my hair, finger curling like my life depended on it. I'd tried every version of curl friendly styling to tame my nest of hair with varying degrees of success, but most of the time I gelled it to my head in a bun when I needed to look put together. Tonight, I wanted to try something different, and I wasn't about to look too closely at the why of it.

Hint: It had nothing to do with impressing investors.

With a defeated sigh, I pushed my hair back off my face and threaded a pair of gold hoops through my ears. My makeup was minimal, as usual, because it was hard as hell to do anything fancy with glasses on, and I couldn't see anything without them.

The dress would do most of the work tonight, though. I'd complimented my hair with a figure-hugging forest green number that had cost more than I'd ever confidently spend on myself. The sweetheart neckline toed the line between modest and daring. I loved it. Professional and classy in a way I just couldn't pull off day to day.

Some lavender essential oils on pulse points to help with anxiety and to smell pretty, and I was ready to go.

As I searched my closet for my black stilettos, a knock echoed through my apartment. The clock read seven PM. Nice to know Cian O'Leary was a man of his word. Stepping into the foot-prisons, I grabbed my purse and hustled for the front door. Just before I opened things up, I realized my cell was still on charge.

"Hey, come in, I just have to grab something," I said, heading for the bedroom before I'd pulled the door all the way open.

"Okay." The door clicked shut behind him.

Cian O'Leary is in my apartment.

Putting on a little more speed so he wasn't left to his own devices for too long, I grabbed my phone, almost tearing the charger out of the wall in my rush. As I stumbled, my shoe slipped off, hitting the floorboards with a clatter.

"Nice place," he called from somewhere over near my sofa.

"Oh, thanks. It's not much, but it's enough." I hopped a few steps, trying to slip my foot into the shoe. My body tipped on my single point of balance and I threw out a hand and slapped the wall to avoid a face plant.

I hated dressing up.

With a sigh, I slid the stupid shoe on and straightened my dress, then went to confront the night I'd somehow committed myself to.

My footsteps announced my arrival in the sitting area, the clipping loud in the open space. Cian looked over from the photo he'd been studying—one of me in pee wee hockey—and smiled.

"I thought you might have played."

At least... that's what I thought he said. My mind had gone blank at the sight of his stupidly pretty face and body jacked into a freaking tuxedo. His beard was neatly trimmed and his hair slicked back like a young Colin Farrell. This was exactly why he was dangerous.

"Are you ready to go? You look..." His eyes traveled down my body in a sweep that seemed to catalog every one of my faults.

"Yeah, I know. I did the best I could. Come on, let's go."

I headed for the door but was pulled up short by a grip on my elbow.

Cian was far too close, his eyes burning with something I didn't want to read into.

"You look amazing, Blair. Really pretty."

"Whatever." I shrugged out of his grip and stepped out into the hall, waiting for him to follow me before I locked up.

We took the stairs in silence, our footsteps echoing in the tight space, and as we stepped out into the evening air, I breathed in deeply. This was my favorite time of day. When the sun was close to the horizon and the heat of the day had banked from searing down to something that felt comforting. Cozy. We were close enough to the Colorado River that the musty, slightly fishy smell lingered on the breeze.

"I'm over here." Cian gestured toward a huge black truck that I'd seen in the parking lot enough to recognize.

"Compensating for something?" I muttered, eyeing the door and wondering how the hell I'd be able to climb up in my dress. The gasp behind me was as unexpected as the light hand that cupped my elbow almost solicitously. "Why, Miss Kennedy. I am shocked and appalled that you would question my manhood. Besides, we're still getting to know each other. I'm not *that* kind of girl." Ridiculously long lashes framed his comically–widened olive eyes, and if it were anyone else, I would have laughed. Instead, I pushed him away, feigning irritation, and closed the distance to his truck.

"Do you have a stepladder for this thing?"

He reached past me to unlock the passenger door and wrapped his hands around my hips.

"No, but I can lift you."

His grip was warm and overly familiar. Long fingers that almost met at my belly button made me feel almost dainty. This close, his cologne filled my nose. A spicy scent that made me a little dizzy and a lot aware of his proximity.

With an ease that I refused to admit was a turn on, he lifted me into the passenger seat and stepped back, eyes intense on mine.

A generic red sports car pulled in on the other side of the lot, and I took the excuse to break away from whatever this moment was.

The driver stepped out and slammed the door behind him, rubbing a hand on his worn jeans as he spoke into this cell.

"Yeah, I just got here. Nah, just a Netflix and chill thing with some chick whose mom set us up." He laughed. "Oh, no way. Hopefully, I'll get my dick sucked and come meet you guys later."

"Oh shit," I hissed, realizing who the obnoxious blond was. "Get in. We've gotta go."

Cian's brow furrowed, like he hadn't heard a word the idiot across the way had spoken.

Worried we'd be spotted, I leaned in close, slapped my hands to his cheeks and spoke slowly. "Please get in the car right now. I don't want to deal with that." I turned his head in Scott's direction and suppressed a shudder as he checked his breath and pressed my apartment's call button.

"He's here for you?"

"No, he's here because my mother has control issues. Now, please." I gestured at the driver's door, and Cian finally got with the program.

"Thank you, God," I muttered as my... work colleague slid into the truck. He reversed carefully out of the parking slot before peeling away from my apartment complex, leaving the asshole with big oral aspirations holding his metaphorical dick in his hand. The mental image was so absurd a giggle burst out. Cian glanced over with a small grin, and I lost it. Like an inmate pardoned from death row, I cackled at the close call. Relief flooded through my system, and I couldn't even find it in me to hate that my salvation had come at the hands of Cian O'Leary. The man in question watched me with a bewildered little quirk to his lips as I did my best impression of a hyena.

Damn, my laugh was unattractive.

Cian navigated us smoothly through Austin traffic, and I settled into a content silence. It was weirdly comfortable sitting beside him in the truck, and I tried to discreetly study the hockey player I'd made it my mission to hate.

One of his large hands rested on the top of the steering wheel, altering our position on the road with little pushes of the heel that shouldn't have been as sexy as it was. His other hand shifted between the stick shift and his knee, tapping out the rhythm of the song playing softly over the radio. His shoulders were relaxed, eyes flicking between the road and rearview with a calm confidence that made me want to sink further into the soft seat.

The growing peace was broken by a loud buzzing in my purse.

My phone.

It was my mom. I knew this without looking because I wasn't complying with her directive for the night. Even if Scott hadn't called her, she had a sixth sense for this kind of thing.

We coasted to a stop at a traffic light, and Cian glanced over.

"Are you going to get that?"

I kept my eyes forward and gave my head a small shake, hoping we would get moving again, like we could outpace the call if we had a clear run. Cars shot across the intersection in front of us. Everyone was in a rush to get somewhere, all those cars only impacted us so much as their passage hindered our own.

"It's my mom." I didn't know why I felt the need to share that tidbit. Cian was a work colleague who I didn't like, but in this space with him, I felt inexplicably safe. "I hate her."

"Your mom?"

I nodded, and when that didn't feel like enough, I gave him a tight smile.

"It's okay, she hated me first."

Cars slowed on either side of the intersection. The lights changed. His stare burned into the side of my head.

"The light's green."

Without a word, he put the truck in gear and didn't slow until we pulled into the parking lot of the function.

The event passed in a blur of hand shaking, sparkling wine, and fake smiles for deep pocketed patrons. By the time the silent auction was drawn, my feet ached and I'd developed a muscle tick in my right cheek.

I hated these things, but they were part of the job, and a vindictive part of me usually got enjoyment out of making Cian do them too. He was an action kind of guy who had no patience for the forced pleasantries. But tonight felt different. It could have been arriving together, or maybe that moment in the car, or perhaps how he had checked in on me so solicitously throughout the night, but as he grimaced his way through a conversation with an older couple whose eyes shone with an uncomfortable greed, I felt drawn to his side.

"Please excuse me," I told them, tucking my hand into his elbow. "I need to borrow Mr. O'Leary."

I pulled him away to a chorus of vaguely hostile agreement and well wishes for the season.

"Thank you. I'm pretty sure they were gearing up to ask for a ménage á trois."

"They were ancient!"

"Little blue pills and lube solve a multitude of problems."

I pulled us to a stop, gaping at him until I noticed a small tick in the corner of his lips.

"You jerk!" I slapped his shoulder. "I thought you were serious."

He chuckled, steering me toward the exit with subtle movements.

"Seriously, though. They seemed a little intense."

He nodded, opening the door and guiding me through with a hand on my lower back that burned through my dress.

"I'm used to it. You actually saved me before the inappropriate comments started, so thanks for that." He smiled at me as we wandered out into the warm night air. A part of me couldn't believe I was speaking so easily with the man I'd hated for so long.

And then he went and ruined things.

"Oh, hey. I forgot to show you. I wore these just for you." Pausing in the middle of the parking lot, he hitched up his pant leg to display socks with little rubber duckies stitched into them. "Get it? Duckies. Like you."

How did he know about the nickname? Had this all been a setup to remind me that I would always be the ugly fucking duckling?

My stomach churned as he waited for a response. What the hell could I say?

With a deep breath through my nose, I blinked against the burning behind my eyes.

"Message received. Take me home, please." There. Polite, without showing how much it hurt.

Why did I think it was a good idea to trust him with anything? He'd already proven it was a bad idea.

Because I was attracted to him.

Despite how he'd treated me years ago, my *not-good-enough-ugly* heart had decided it wanted him.

"Wait, what? What message?" His brow furrowed as he, thankfully, dropped his pant leg back over the stupid socks. I rolled my eyes and bee-lined for his truck. I still had my dignity, dammit, and I didn't have to stick around and be the butt of anyone else's jokes. That was the beauty of being an adult, you chose the company you kept.

"Hey, I'm sorry I upset you. I didn't mean to…" He cut off with a sigh as I resolutely stared at the locked door of his truck.

When the locks clicked open, he reached to lift me into

his truck but I brushed his hands away and awkwardly climbed in by myself.

On the drive home, I steadfastly ignored the looks he cast my way. He didn't get to fuck with my head and then demand answers. If I thought the sudden rift between us would cause even a second of lost sleep for him I might have felt guilty, but Cian would forget about me and my hurt little feelings the second he dropped me in front of my apartment building.

As soon as the truck pulled to a stop in my parking lot, I slid out the door, nearly twisting an ankle on the way down, but nothing would stop me getting inside. Back to safety. The thunk behind me told me Cian had jumped out to walk me to my door, unexpected, and extremely unwelcome. I was done. The burning in my eyes had evolved into a well of tears that blurred my vision, and I'd be goddamned if he saw even one of them.

My keys were in the bottom of my purse, evading my grip as I lengthened my stride.

"Blair." He was close behind me. Of course. He had stupidly long legs and wasn't trying to make an escape in stilettos. My fingertips brushed the key set, and I grasped it like a lifeline.

"What?!" My voice cracked.

There was a moment of silence where our the click of my heels and the clomp of his shoes echoed around the parking lot in a synchronized symphony of unsaid words, and I had to work at not turning around.

"I'm scared anything I say to you will make it worse," he said. His footsteps slowed to a stop, still a distance back as I reached my door and spent no time unlocking it.

. . .

"Good night, Cian." I spared a single glance back as I slipped inside, barely able to stand the way his eyebrows furrowed. The downturn of his soft mouth.

He looked almost... confused. But that wasn't right. He'd intentionally humiliated me with the reminder of the awful nickname that I thought I'd left with my family.

Apparently not.

CHAPTER
SIX

Cian

I HADN'T SLEPT in two nights. Ok... so I'd slept, of course I had. Between training camp and the start of the preseason, I needed the rest, but I hadn't slept well. My first attempt at being Blair's friend had been a bust, and I had no idea why.

So, I was going to speak to an expert.

I let myself into Mia and Oscar's house, praying she was home and could put that fancy psychology degree to use and help me.

"Mia."

"In here." The reply came from the living room. I dragged myself through the house and found her curled up on the sofa. She smiled in welcome and put aside her book. "What's up?"

I groaned. Crossing the room, I flopped beside her, dropping my head in her lap. Her arms floated above me, wavering slightly as though unsure where to rest.

"What are you doing?" she asked.

"I feel bad. I need comfort. And your brain."

"My brother is literally touch averse. Oscar's the cuddly one. Can't you find someone else to do this?"

I probably could, but the fact that Mia was not only trained as a psychologist, but also hadn't had a great upbringing gave me hope she'd be able to help me figure this out. She settled her hand lightly on my shoulder, resigning herself to the contact.

"Where is Oscar, by the way?" I decided to push my luck, taking her other hand and encouraging her to scratch my head. It felt nice, and when she continued to do it after I took my hand away, I let out a shuddering breath. I'd always been a touchy kind of person; it was another reason Oscar and I always got on so well. A bro hug could heal all manner of ills. Human contact was critical to wellbeing.

"He's helping his mom for the weekend." Oscar's mom was awesome, even if his sisters were a little scary. Tia wasn't too bad, she'd been a soccer queen before her injury, but Elle was downright terrifying when she was in a mood. Usually, Mia wouldn't miss the opportunity to hang out with all of them.

"Why didn't you go with him?"

"I have to work."

I smirked, unable to help myself. "Oh yeah, how is it being a madam?" The first time Oscar and I had met Mia, she was dancing in a burlesque revue. There was nothing seedy about the venues Mia performed in, but it was still fun to tease her about it.

"I'm managing a burlesque show, not a brothel."

"Same difference."

"Get out." Neither of us moved.

"Don't be like that. Oscar would love me in my time of need."

Mia huffed and started running her nails through my hair. Hell yes, this was nice.

"He'll be home next week."

"But I need comfort now! Why is she like this?"

"Okay, let's start with a name."

Oh yeah. As briefly as possible, I ran over the details of the night before, and Blair's general dislike of me. I'd thought things were going really well until they just... weren't.

"You can't make everyone like you. You may just have to accept she's one of the ones who you can't win over."

Something turned in my gut, and I scowled at the idea of not seeing Blair smile again.

"There has to be something. Like, how did I mess up last night? I thought it was going well."

Mia mulled it over for a moment. The gentle scrape of her nails over my scalp soothed me, and I thought back to when I picked Blair up the night before. That dress had been killer, hugging her curves in a way that bordered on obscene. I hadn't lied when I said she looked good.

"Okay, I have to ask something before we keep talking about this."

I shifted my head to see her better, silently cursing when she stopped the stroking. Her brows were furrowed; her bottom lip caught between her teeth.

"Oscar told me about the bet with Doyle." Her voice dropped as she said his name. As much as the team disliked him, the PASs — partners and spouses — hated him more.

"Are you trying to get close to her just to win it?"

I sat up so quickly I almost fell off the sofa. Whipping around to face her, I studied her face closely. Did she really think so little of me?

"I don't care about that stupid bet. I only agreed so he

would shut up because Blair didn't need to hear him running his mouth about her. I want to be her friend, but she hates me, and I don't know why."

"Why do you think it's so important to you that the two of you are friends?"

What kind of question was that?

"We work together. It's important to get along with the people you work with."

Mia snorted, then covered her nose with a hand, silver eyes dancing with something close to amusement. "Well, that's not true. For one thing, no one gets along with Chet. You all barely tolerate him, and you play together just fine. For another thing, you've told me that Blair is always professional in the workplace. Your social media profile is as well put together as anyone else in the team's. So try again. Why do you think it's important?"

"She's smart, she's funny, she knows stats better than anyone I've ever met. The first time I met her, I felt like I already knew her, which was really weird because it was hate at first sight for her." Why did it matter so much that she and I were friends? I'd been working for years on my people pleasing tendencies, and clung hard to the mantra *stop trying to make everyone like you. You don't even like everyone.* But it was different with Blair. It felt like we should be friends. And I'd tried to give her space. I had. But I was done with just standing back and dealing with it alone.

"Is it possible that you like Blair?" Mia asked gently.

"Of course I like her. That's why I want to be friends with her."

She shook her head, an affectionate smile on her face that made me feel like an ignorant kid.

"Cian. Is there a chance you'd like to date Blair, and the hostility is uncomfortable because you want her?"

"I don't... she's not..." I huffed. How could I explain this without sounding like a complete asshole. Luckily, this was Mia.

"She's not conventionally attractive, no. But is that what matters to you? I've seen you turn down gorgeous puck bunnies because you care more about other people's wellbeing than you do about cheap thrills."

Shit, maybe Mia's insight was a little more than I could handle. Heat burned up the back of my neck, and I shifted in my seat.

"You're a good-looking guy who is used to being surrounded by good-looking people. But looks fade, and what's most important is who you are at your core. I love Oscar because he's a cinnamon roll of a human being who understands me like no one else. He's a proud feminist who is terrified of birds to the point of being ridiculous, and I know that there's nothing he wouldn't do to make sure I'm happy and safe every day of our lives. The fact that he's six foot four inches of muscle with a pretty face is nice, but it was never the reason I chose him."

I'd never bought into the puck bunny culture because it felt transactional. Having a beautiful girl hanging off you for the night so she could be seen with someone considered a celebrity, and in exchange getting off with a stranger at the end of the night. It felt hollow. Cheap and nasty and nothing like what I wanted for the future. Did that mean I wanted Blair?

I wasn't sure because I'd never considered it.

Talk about shallow.

"I think you need to take some time to decide what your

motivation is behind all this. If you want to be her friend, act like it. If she doesn't want that, then respect her boundary. That's part of being an adult, and it's unfair to drag her into something just because you want it a certain way. But if you genuinely want to have something more with her..." She trailed off, watching me intently. "Well, you're Cian O'Leary. I don't think there's anything you can't achieve if you put your mind to it. Just make sure you're doing it for the right reasons."

I pushed to my feet, mind churning. I wanted to make a friendship with Blair work. Was that selfish? Probably. But we'd both seemed to have fun at the function until...

"Where do you think I went wrong on Friday? I still can't work it out."

Mia glanced up from her book. "Do you know how she got the nickname Duckie?"

I'd assumed it was a term of endearment by her family. The image of Blair sitting in my truck flashed through my mind along with her heartbreaking words. *It's okay, she hated me first.* Shit.

"I thought it was like how ducks always look calm on the water, but underneath they're paddling like hell. Blair is so capable that she never seems ruffled, even though her job gets crazy a lot of the time."

Mia shrugged, giving me a soft smile before she dropped her eyes to her book. I knew I'd been dismissed, but she couldn't do all my thinking for me.

I had to figure this out on my own.

CHAPTER
SEVEN

Blair

"THE USUAL?" Toni asked as I stumbled into the Wild Brew Cafe.

"Please." I dropped into a chair to wait for my caffeine fix. Preseason had been a blur of wins, marred only by a last-minute loss to St. Louis in the final period. The team was in a good place heading into the official season, and we were due to fly out to Nashville in three hours. I'd stopped by the office to get my tablet and was unable to resist the call of coffee.

"You look tired." Toni's eyes were assessing as she watched me from over the top of her espresso machine. I hoped I'd be able to find a decent coffee while we were away because she was right. I hadn't been sleeping well. Or at all, really.

"Nah, that's just my face," I joked, waving a hand at her. Rather than the laugh I was expecting, she hummed, a small crease forming between her brows.

"You do that a lot, you know?"

"What?" I asked, eyeing the steam from the frothing wand as it disappeared into the milk jug.

"You use self-deprecating humor. Be careful, that shit is a slippery slope. Trust me. You'll start believing it after a while and life gets harder than it needs to be."

This didn't feel like the usual barista/customer conversation. Although, I'd built somewhat of a friendship with her over the last year.

"I'm just saying what everyone else is thinking," I said, shrugging it off. The frothing wand choked off with an indignant squeal. Toni dropped the milk jug against the counter in a couple of loud thumps and narrowed her eyes at me.

"No one is thinking that except you, baby girl. How about you try being nice to yourself once in a while and see if things change?"

I really didn't want to be a part of this conversation. People had tried this whole *self-love* thing on me before. I much preferred when people had the guts to tell me the truth instead of some pretty lie. Instead of engaging with her, I drummed my fingers against my thigh as she poured the milk into my latte and sealed the lid.

"Thanks." I almost snatched the cup from her hand as she offered it up.

"Have a good trip," she called after me as I hustled out the door and across the road to where Dante waited, looking as put together as always.

"Ready to go?" she asked, picking up her overnight bag as our Uber pulled up. Dante didn't have scrappy old bags with shoulder straps and suspicious stains like us mere humans. She had a tote bag with handles that seemed to mold perfectly to her hands. I bet her clothing was folded in some Marie Kondo perfect origami that kept it from wrinkling.

"I just have to grab my bag." I popped the trunk on my car and grabbed my own overnight bag—my old hockey kit bag, because I broke the tote I'd bought for overnight trips and hadn't had a chance to replace it yet.

Dante slid smoothly into the backseat of the Uber, and I joined her a moment later.

"How are you feeling after preseason?" she asked as we moved through the light Friday morning traffic.

"Good. There's so much more to the PR stuff than I thought, but I'm excited to learn it all. How's Miller?" Dante had been checking in with the second line winger after his apartment building caught fire the previous week. Per his request, she kept news of the incident from becoming public knowledge and we had run a player spotlight campaign for good measure to distract the media. Dante was a PR goddess, and I was starting to worry about how I could step into her shoes next year. If I got the job, that was.

"He's good. Off the record, he's moved in with a teammate, so at least he has somewhere to crash until he can find somewhere new."

I nodded absently, my mind wandering to another of his teammates who had taken up far too much of my thoughts lately.

Since the night of the function, I'd attempted to go back to our status quo: only interacting when strictly necessary for my job. But he had started turning up at the most random times. For someone who should have been focusing on his preseason games, he apparently had plenty of time to appear when I least expected it with a second coffee he'd *accidentally* bought. It was kind, and considerate, and suspicious as fuck.

What did he want from me?

The question played on my mind until we pulled up to the air strip. The team milled about on the tarmac in their suits, all of them looking ready for a GQ photoshoot while some diehard fans tried to get their attention from the other side of the fence. The airline ground staff hustled about, doing preflight checks and positioning the airstairs before rounding up the team for boarding. Spencer Cotton, the owner of the Austin Aces, boarded first. He flew with the team whenever his schedule allowed and took the front of the airplane as his office for the duration of the flight. The coaches filed on next, along with the film crew, who were shadowing the team for the season. Next was the team, and Dante and I realized our mistake at the same moment. Casting a glance at my mentor, I blanched at the rueful smile on her face.

"I guess we're running the gauntlet," she muttered, placing her sensible heel on the bottom step with a sigh.

The team had very strict dress rules when it came to traveling to and from games, and the guys took these rules seriously. Nicely pressed slacks, shirts and jackets at all times. In order to maintain the standard of dress expected, the second the guys stepped foot on the plane, they would strip down to boxers and neatly hang their suits.

Sure enough, as soon as we passed through the door, making room for flight staff to close things up behind us and start safety checks, we were confronted with a labyrinth of half-naked men. Closest to us was Adam Riley, one of the rookies I'd met during the development camp in July, whose face flushed scarlet as he straightened with dress pants in hand and tried to shuffle aside to make room for us to pass.

"It's all right. We'll wait," Dante assured him with a professional smile.

"Hurry up and take your seats so we can get moving," Mack called over the dull roar of conversation that almost drowned out the sound of the engines warming up below us. At the order from the head coach, the aisle began to clear. As Oscar's bulk moved aside, I caught sight of a whole lot more bronzed skin than I needed to see. Cian had his broad back to us, clothed in a tight pair of black boxers that left little to the imagination as he pulled a pair of gray sweatpants up his legs. Despite the fact that there were males everywhere in a similar state of undress, seeing him like this felt different.

Look away.

Before I could follow the sage advice, he turned and caught my eye.

Busted.

His chest was even more impressive than his back. Without breaking eye contact, he placed a large hand on a set of rock-hard abs. His shoulder rolled as he rubbed back and forth until I couldn't help but follow the movement. The flex and pull of muscles made me think of how he would move over someone in the bedroom. How those round shoulders would bunch and release while he pumped into... *Stop.*

But damn, his body was perfect.

And I felt like an ass objectifying him like that. Mentally shaking myself, I looked away from the mesmerizing movement and flushed as he winked. As though he knew exactly where my mind had been.

Without bothering to pull on a shirt, he dropped into

the seat next to Oscar, stretching his arms over his head in a way I told myself wasn't for my benefit.

Not at all.

"They're not supposed to be filming this." Dante pushed through the remaining players who hadn't changed fast enough, intent on retaining some level of modesty for the players that they themselves may not have cared about. Then again, maybe they did, and Dante was the only voice they had to advocate for them. Following along more slowly, I weaved my way to where Dante was having a quiet word with the showrunner.

"I want to review the footage before it goes to edits."

"You will," Lily assured her before returning to her seat. Dante waved me into a seat across the way.

"Just because they've been good so far doesn't mean we can trust them. I have to keep our team safe, and it'll be your job to do it in the future. Once photos or footage hit the internet, it's almost impossible to scrub it completely. Prevention is always better than correction."

I nodded along, storing the advice for later as I glanced around the cabin. Flight crew bustled up and down the aisle as players strapped in to their seats, many of them beginning pre-game rituals ranging from meditation to pump up music, while others took the opportunity to nap. On the opposite side of the plane, halfway down in the aisle seat, Cian's head was tilted back, headphones stuck in his ears while his heavy-lidded eyes felt like they burned through me.

His attention was too much. I didn't know why I'd landed on his radar after three years of quietly deciding to be unspoken enemies, but I didn't trust it.

I didn't trust him.

And I really wished he would put a shirt on.

CHAPTER
EIGHT

Cian

I DRUMMED ON THE BOARDS, screaming encouragement as Oscar flew down the ice. Nashville was riding us hard, but no way were we giving up the W in this game. I missed playing on his line, but Miller and Lathan were easy to read, and we worked well together. The lamp lit up and our third line forwards sprinted for the bench while our first line spilled onto the ice.

"Great play, Caveman," I shouted, holding my knuckles out for Oscar to knock. He grinned at the nickname and flopped onto the bench beside me, squirting his water bottle into his mouth without bothering to remove his helmet.

"Shit. How long do we have left on the clock?" he asked, breathing hard. We both grimaced as the Nashville goalie shut out Viggy's slapshot, but Han was already circling the net for another attack.

"You ready?" Lathan thumped me on the shoulder. I

nodded and slid my mouthguard in under my helmet. I was always ready to play. Energy thrummed through my body as play continued in front of us. The puck zipped back and forth between each of the team's defensive zones, but Logan was on his game in goal and hadn't let anything through this whole period. Finally, Coach blew the whistle, and I vaulted over the boards with Lathan and Miller close behind me. Nashville's defensive line was edgy, clearly unhappy with the scoreboard and almost as soon as I hit the ice, I was driven into the boards.

Not happening.

Instead of engaging with the giant left defenseman, I ducked out from underneath him and sprinted over the ice while Murdock sent the biscuit down the line. Miller circled behind Nashville's goal, positioning himself perfectly while Lathan kept their right D-man busy. Leaning into my skates, I angled my body for a shot I didn't intend to take, waiting for the goalie to move before I passed to Miller who used the advantage to score a bar down. The lamp lit up just as the final siren sounded and the arena echoed with shouts and jeers from the crowd. I never got tired of the feeling of winning on the national stage. Camera crews lined the boards while the announcer confirmed the Aces had taken the win.

We skated for the gate, ignoring shouts from the gathered crowd. They could wait for the presser to get their sound bites. I just prayed Blair didn't want me to sit in on it.

Speak of the devil.

Halfway down the tunnel, with the stadium lights shining off her wild curls, Blair's smile was as wide as any of the team's as she snapped candid shots of my teammates. She squealed a laugh as Han gave her a sweaty hug on the way past. Something uncomfortable slid through my gut as I watched the interaction. I'd never noticed her paying attention to him before, but maybe I'd missed something.

Instead of letting the feeling crawl through me, I shook it off, making a beeline for her to get some of that attention she seemed so ready to give.

As she laughed at something Oscar said to her on his way past, I snuck in close to get in her ear.

"Did you enjoy the game?"

She jumped, pressing a hand to her chest as she wheeled toward me. Her brown eyes seemed lighter than normal. A subtle amber color lighting up the center.

"You scared me. Yeah, you guys were great. Keep that up and we'll take home the cup this—Mmph." I slapped a hand over her mouth before she could jinx our whole season.

"Eew, sweaty hands," she groused, wiping the back of her wrist across her lips. Come to think of it, they were quite full. Pink and plump and perfectly shaped for... What was she saying?

Oh. Right.

"You can't jinx the team in the first week of the season. They'll never forgive you. I was just being a good friend."

"A good friend." Her voice had a curiously flat edge to it when she repeated my completely reasonable claim. I knew I was a good friend. I'd been working extra hard since I spoke to Mia. My takeaway was that I hadn't paid enough attention to her needs. Friends were good at looking after one another. Like when Oscar needed a bird decoy. So I'd thought about what I knew about Blair and came up with one absolute. She liked coffee.

She continued to stare at me while the team disappeared down the hall toward the locker rooms.

"We're friends... right?" I didn't like the note of doubt that crept in when I asked it, but maybe I'd read the room wrong.

"No."

Okay, so it had only been in my... Wait.

"Wait. No?"

"No. We're not friends. What made you think we were?"

The answer to that was simple. I wanted to be. But as I thought more about what Mia had actually said, I realized I hadn't taken Blair's thoughts into account at all.

Although, I was certain she'd been imagining some very friendly things when we were on the plane earlier in the day.

"I'm going to be your friend."

Fuck. I sounded like I was in middle school when I said it like that. But something in me wouldn't let it go. So, I would earn her trust, whatever it took.

"Sure. Good luck with that, big guy." Blair patted my shoulder and headed off toward the locker rooms without a backward glance.

MY COCK THROBBED *in time to the pounding of my heart as hair the color of a banked fire dragged across my chest. The scent of fresh roasted coffee beans filled my nose with a hint of sweetness to take the edge off. With a deep groan, I fisted those curly locks, guiding that soft mouth to the spot I needed her to go. A deep, feminine chuckle ghosted across the tip of my erection, denying me the pleasure I sought. Of course she was a tease.*

This thing between us had been going on a lot longer than either of us had realized.

"Please." The word came out on a hiss as she stroked her tongue along the groove of my hip. So close.

"Do you still think we're friends?"

"I'd do anything to make it friends with benefits right now."

She hummed, and the vibration shot straight through me, taking me right to the edge.

I tried to guide her head the rest of the way, but her hair was no longer in my fist.

She stood over my body, gloriously naked, but somehow blurred. Her silhouette was exactly as I remembered it when I'd held her for that brief moment, but I couldn't see details.

"You're so beautiful," I murmured, palming my erection and giving it a few pumps to relieve the ache.

She dropped to her knees, hovering over my fist as she leaned in and took my earlobe between her teeth.

"Liar."

She sat down hard, taking me all the way inside her.

I came awake with a shout, my body shuddering through an orgasm like a preteen, whose balls had just dropped. What the fuck kind of twenty-six-year-old had a wet dream? I glared at my dick like it was personally responsible for my dreams.

Seriously, dude?

I hadn't forgotten the star of the dream, either. It was all Mia's fault for putting the thought in my mind. Blair was someone I'd like to pursue a friendship with, not a relationship.

"Get that through your thick head," I growled at my rapidly deflating erection. In the dream, it had felt so right, but as the cum dried on my sheets and the sweat slicked my skin, I wanted nothing more than a shower.

CHAPTER
NINE

Cian

"O'Malley's for after game drinks!" The call went up in the locker room as the team buzzed with our fourth victory of the season. San Jose had fought hard, and I had the bruises to prove it, but they came undone in the final period. Laughter echoed around the shower stalls as we released the adrenaline of the game with banter and predictions for the season.

"Are you coming out?" I asked Oscar as he peeled his undershirt away his body. He let the sopping fabric slap to the ground. I grimaced as I dropped my own on top of it.

"I'll check what Mia's doing, but I'm keen. You in?"

"Yeah. I might see if..." I trailed off, wondering if I should finish the thought with so many ears around.

"Do it. Mia's been asking to meet her."

"It's not anything. I just want to be her friend."

Oscar gave me a look I pointedly ignored as I focused on removing my socks.

"Guys and girls can be friends, you know."

"Yeah, but if the girl says no and you keep going... Man, there's a thin line between persistence and stalking."

"I'm not stalking her!"

Locker room, idiot.

"I'm not stalking her," I muttered, stripping off my boxers and wrapping a towel around my waist.

"Look, I'm thoroughly enjoying all the angst. I've never seen anyone get under your skin like this, but for her sake, will you figure out what you want? And don't tell me it's to be friends."

This conversation was going nowhere and my skin felt tight with dried sweat. Time for a shower. Instead of answering him, I grabbed my shower gel and headed for the first available stall. Being a people person meant that I liked making friends. The fact that I couldn't let go of the idea of Blair and I getting closer was commentary on what a cool person she was. No ulterior motives here, I just didn't want her to hate me anymore.

Twenty minutes later, clean and feeling a lot more human, I found her outside the locker room talking in a low voice with Ethan Harrison.

"I just need you to post regularly on your account. I send you the content, but I can't physically hit post for you. Your fans want to see *you* on their feed. Yes, it seems like it's going through the motions, but I promise it'll help."

Ethan's head was bent, folding his six foot two frame down so that Blair didn't draw attention to them. His hands were tucked in his pockets and everything about his posture screamed wanting to be anywhere but here.

Maybe I should have let her keep on him, but seeing as I

had several days of posts sitting in my own inbox to go up, I decided to help him out. I was a nice guy like that.

"Hey man." I slapped him on the shoulder, dividing a smile between them. "You headed to O'Malley's?"

Ethan straightened and shrugged. The tension slid out of his features and seemed to channel into Blair's.

"Maybe. I'll see how I'm feeling."

"Good. Good." Blair's hair was its usual chaos of curls, like a windstorm in fall. But there were dark smudges beneath her chocolate and toffee eyes. The season was tough on us, but sometimes I thought the support staff had it harder. Maybe I should have offered to drive her home and let her sleep, but she didn't seem to socialize with anyone outside of work.

When she waved, I realized Ethan had taken the opportunity to duck away, but I was still stuck on her.

"So, are you coming?"

She turned back to me with a small crease between her brows.

"To O'Malley's," I clarified, stepping a little closer and inhaling the lavender scent that always lingered around her.

"I have a lot to do," she hedged, glancing down the corridor.

"Come on. Just for a little while. You deserve a break, and I know the guys would love to see you there." I wanted her there, but I wasn't sure if that fact would be a help or a reason for her to bail. Blair lifted a hand, her fingers hovering above my chest like she wasn't sure whether to push me away. A half step closed the distance, and I leaned in toward her ear, my voice dropping to that point in my chest where her hand warmed me.

"Live a little." The challenge was an invitation for so

much more. Blair's eyes flared with surprise, her fingers flexing against my shirt as her mouth parted with a small gasp.

"I'll even drive you, if you want to have a drink." I hated that I couldn't tell whether I was winning her over or failing miserably. All I knew was that her hand was still on my pec, and I didn't want her to let go.

She startled, her gaze dropping to her hip where my hand had come to rest. Huh. I gave a little squeeze, then let it drop as she put some unneeded distance between us.

"I'll meet you there."

"Bet." I grinned, hoping to cover the small shot of disappointment I felt. She rejected the ride but agreed to hang out. Small wins.

Her lips quirked as she took another step back before turning away.

"I'll buy you a drink," I called, definitely not watching how her ass moved in the tight pair of jeans she'd worn for the game. I loved how casually she dressed for her job. Not that Dante didn't look badass in her power suits, but Blair could be comfortable and still hand the guys their balls. No costumes needed.

"Stop looking at my ass," she called over her shoulder as she reached a junction in the hallway.

The comment was so unexpected that a laugh bubbled out before I could stop it.

"What if I say no?"

She turned the corner without reply, and I found myself walking a little faster than necessary back to the locker room to grab my gear and head out.

A mile from Austin Arena, O'Malley's Irish Pub was an institution in Aces culture. Owned by former player, Tadhg

Murphy, it was the preferred meeting place for social events and aftergame hangouts.

Standing room only took on a whole new meaning as I pushed through the door and had to sidestep the crush of bodies lined up to order at the bar.

The aftergame wrap-up was blaring from the television mounted behind the bar, barely audible over the eighties rock ballad pumping through speakers.

Between the noise, the press of bodies, and the stink of sweat and stale beer, it was a sensory overload that brought on nostalgic thoughts of college coupled with a trauma response to playing hungover in the first year before I decided I wanted hockey more than I wanted to get wasted.

It was all fun and games until you vomited on the ice.

Twice in one week.

Coach had rightly torn me a new asshole and told me in no uncertain terms I could be the player who makes captain, or the wasted talent who got benched.

No brainer, really.

"Oh, thank God. It's packed in here."

I blinked out of my memories, slowly registering the small hand on my arm.

She came.

"Come on, they keep tables for us at the back." Using the crowd as an excuse, I gripped Blair's hand and tugged her through the crowd. The going was slow as every second person stopped to ask me for photos, or congratulate me on the team's win, but I kept hold of her hand through all of it.

"I can get through by myself," she grumbled as yet another person called my name. She tugged against my grip halfheartedly.

Instead of stopping, I raised a hand at the guy who wanted my attention and reeled Blair in closer, taking a risk by placing a hand on her lower back and guiding her to where several tables had been pushed together and several of my teammates were already passing around jugs of beer.

"Look who I found," I announced, presenting Blair like her arrival was a happy accident. Oscar waved us over to a couple of vacant seats across from him and Mia.

"Glad you could make it. This is my wife, Mia," he said to her as soon as we were in earshot. I pulled a chair out for her, ignoring the suspicious look she shot me, and waited until she sat down with a huff.

"Nice to meet you, Mia," she said as I grabbed two clean glasses from the center of the table and filled them, passing one to Blair like it was something I did all the time. She accepted the drink with barely a glance as she launched into a conversation with Mia about her psychology degree and burlesque dancing while I watched her quietly, enjoying seeing her relax and open up. Her grin sparkled as she laughed at something Oscar said, and I offered a refill on her glass as she drained the last of it.

She nodded, leaning in until her lips brushed my ear.

"Thank you for inviting me out. I'm having fun."

I wasn't sure whether she knew her hand was on my thigh, but the heat of it went straight to my dick, making my jeans tight.

"Cian O'Leary?"

I mentally cursed as Blair sat back, a blonde woman filling the space between us.

Not a woman. A puck bunny.

Ok, so she was a woman, that wasn't fair, but I really wanted...

"What?"

"Can I get a photo with you?"

"Oh, yeah. Sure." I pushed back my chair to stand and

instead ended up with a lap full of hockey fan. I shifted to make sure she didn't land on my rapidly deflating problem, then put one hand on the table and the other on the back of the chair. Hands always in sight was a fundamental rule of fan photos. Always keep things chaste and stay beyond reproach.

She took a lifetime to get the 'right' photo, turning this way and that, checking each shot like it would be submitted for a Pulitzer.

"Okay, I think we got it," I grumbled as she sank further into my lap, like she was making herself comfortable.

"It doesn't have to end here," she said, leaning in until we were chest to chest. "I can be very good for you." In case I missed her intent, she licked her lips and slid a hand down my chest.

"I'm good." I caught her wrist and used it to help her to stand.

Once free, I leaned around her body to get back to my conversation with the woman I actually wanted to talk to.

The chair beside me was empty.

Blair

THE WINNING streak lasted until game five of the season. We were in Washington, and even from the sidelines, the game was a bloodbath.

Washington's left D man was a mucker who seemed to have it out for Cian, the two having to be pulled apart twice before the end of the first period and the distraction cost the team. I'd never seen Cian anything less than completely in control on the ice, but when he missed a shot late in the third period, he looked ready to explode as he chewed his mouthguard and took up position.

Of course, I'd accepted when he invited me out with the team afterward. His smile had been a little more forced than usual, unlike mine when he took my hand to guide me to the table the team had claimed close to the back.

And of course, I left as soon as the puck bunnies turned up and Cian's focus shifted to better options.

He kept calling us friends, and a good friend didn't

cockblock their friend when they were staying out of town and needed comfort after a difficult loss. Maybe one of them could ice his bruises for him. Strip him out of that olive green shirt that so perfectly matched his eyes and make him forget with their mouths and...

Stop it.

I shook the thoughts of what Cian could be up to out of my head and refocused on the behind-the-scenes footage I was putting together to post on the team's social page. I had a cute clip of Oscar and our equipment manager, Toby Miller, goofing off with a soccer ball, and another of our rookie, Riley, finding his locker full of rolls and rolls of stick tape.

I took a sip of the horrible instant coffee I'd made out of desperation and pulled up the next file when a knock at the door broke my concentration. The clock read one AM, and I wondered if someone had gotten their room number wrong. Maybe one of the players had locked themselves out of their room and no other staff member answered their door? Or shit had hit the fan and Dante wanted me to sit in while she ran damage control.

It was the last possibility that forced me out of my seat to see who my early-early morning visitor was.

A waft of alcohol hit me in the face as I opened the door to over six feet of unsteady man. His hair was disheveled like he—or someone else—had been running their fingers through it. His eyes were bloodshot, face soft in the way of the inebriated. T-shirt and jeans were in place, though the former was untucked and ruched up over one hip.

"Where are your shoes?" I asked. Formerly white socks peeped out below the denim cuffs of his pants, and the toes in them wiggled as he dropped his head with a frown.

"Huh."

He scrunched his toes a few more times, but otherwise seemed content to stand at my door in the middle of the night with no explanation.

His huge body swayed slightly like he was caught in a windstorm, but couldn't take shelter. I leaned out into the hallway, checking both ends in hopes one of his teammates were coming to retrieve their wayward brother. Other than the flickering exit sign down on the left, nothing moved.

What had happened since I left? Cian was always up for being social, but he rarely drank to excess, especially when we had an early flight and another game in two days' time.

"Why are you here?" I asked, torn between letting him in and escorting him to his room. The problem being I wasn't sure exactly where he was staying, and it seemed like a bad idea to have him in my space.

He lurched heavily to the side, knocking his shoulder against the doorframe.

"Shit." I ducked under his arm. God, he was heavier than I expected. As I tried to keep him upright, he curled his big body around me and dropped his face close to mine.

"You're so pretty, Duckie."

That nickname.

I pulled away, almost immediately lunging for him again as he overbalanced.

"Goddamn it, Cian. This is really unfair. You need to go to bed."

He hummed.

Then he stepped into my room.

"You need to go to *your* bed," I stressed, tugging at his arm, which now seemed a hell of a lot steadier. Instead of listening to my very sound advice, he took a seat on my bed and pinned me with eyes that seemed a whole lot more focused all of a sudden.

"You disappeared again."

"I—What?" I asked, unsure what had changed.

"You always disappear on me. I want you to stay." He leaned back on his hands and became distracted by the feel of the bed covers. He kneaded the mattress, eyes focused on his fingers curling in the sheets, then flipped over and crawled up to the pillows.

"This is nice," he muttered, curling on his side as he let out a heavy breath.

"Oh, hell no. You are not sleeping in here. Get out of my bed."

The only answer was a soft snore.

"Oh, for fuck's sake." I crawled up the bed, muttering about stupid drunk hockey players as I pushed at his huge, heavy as hell body. Why was he doing this?

I was sweating and breathing hard a few minutes later when I finally surrendered to the fact I was stuck with this beautiful, confusing, very passed out man in my bed for the foreseeable future. Pushing my curls out of my face with a frustrated hand, I studied his ridiculously long, dark lashes. His face relaxed in sleep, and it was only seeing him like this that made me realize the tension that had been in his features since we boarded the plane yesterday.

Something was on his mind, and as much as I told myself it wasn't my business, I might... possibly... have wanted to make it my business? Maybe?

Despite my best efforts to keep him at arm's length, Cian O'Leary had the kind of charisma that was difficult to resist. He made people want to be near him, and I was getting tired of resisting his charm.

Which was more dangerous than any interaction with my family.

They could hurt me.

Cian O'Leary had the ability to utterly destroy me.

Which was why I called myself every variant of idiot as I put my glasses on the nightstand and curled up beside him to try to get an hour or two of restless sleep.

AN INSISTENT BEEPING broke through my dreamless sleep, and I groaned, silently willing it to shut the hell up. Christ, I was warm. Sweat slid down my back, and I wondered why the hotel had such heavy covers. The bed dipped, and I froze as something large and warm squeezed my breast. Flashes of the night before came back to me as my brain woke up. Something else was clearly awake, and as I tried to shift away from the hockey player wrapped around me, I felt it slide against my ass cheeks.

"Cian."

With a sleepy grunt, he hooked his leg over my hip and pulled me more tightly against him. His hips ground lazily into my ass as he buried his face in the back of my neck. Goosebumps raced along my skin as his hot breath coasted over my ear. The small snuffling noises he made in his sleepy state were not cute. At all. Really.

Maybe I could let him sleep just a little longer.

My alarm chose that moment to voice its opinion, recommencing the beep beeping with every increasing volume until my bedmate came away with a rough curse. Without releasing his hold on me, he reached out a hand and silenced the beeping, then curled his body back around me.

The tension in his body a moment later told me when he came fully awake.

The hand on my breast squeezed once before taking a

lazy stroke down my body, up over my hip and finally settled in my hair, moving it away from his face.

"Blair?" he asked quietly.

"Uh... hi?"

He pulled his hips, and that erection I was quietly curious about, away from me with such a violent jerk he threw himself off the bed. The crash of his landing was accompanied by the bedside lamp following him down, as well as half the bedding. With a less-than-graceful push, he found his feet and flapped around, trying to untangle the sheets from his body. While he fought, I retrieved my glasses from the nightstand. Without them, I couldn't see a whole lot more than color and blurred shapes.

"What are you doing in my room?" he asked, finally free of his restraints and sporting a deep crease between his brows.

"Actually, you're in my room," I said, pointing to my laptop as though it were proof of residence.

He looked around the small space that was mine for the night we'd spent in Washington. It wasn't as fancy as where the players slept, and after the night we'd had, I would have appreciated something bigger than a double bed, but it was enough for me to get my work done. Cian's expression told me he may not have agreed.

"What am I doing in your room?" he asked at last.

"Do you remember anything from last night?"

He kicked the sheets away and paced in the small space, hands on hips and head bowed.

"You left again."

"You said that last night."

He nodded, his movements becoming more sure. "You do that a lot. Come out with us for a drink, but as soon as my back is turned, you ghost. Why do you keep leaving?"

"I know when I'm not wanted."

"You...? Are you serious right now?" He may have been the color of flour and smelled like stale booze, but Cian in a mood still cut an intimidating figure.

He stalked forward, until he stood over me on the bed.

"What part of the night made you feel unwanted? Was it when I explicitly invited you? When I held your hand and sat you beside me? Maybe when I made sure we both had drinks because I'd had a really shitty night and wanted you close. Tell me, Blair. When were you not wanted?"

I lifted my chin and met his glare, kind of wishing I could stand up and meet him eye to eye, but he didn't give me the space for that.

"When better options came along."

He opened his mouth. Closed it. Rubbed his hand down his face and winced like his head hurt.

"I'm too hungover for this," he muttered. "What 'better options' came along?" He crooked two fingers as he spoke, turning the sentence into a quote.

Heat flooded my face. Did he want me to spell it out for him?

"Those puck bunnies are always so accommodating for you. It looked like you'd used them well before you came looking for the last resort. Should I thank you for giving me a look in?"

"What...?"

"You know. The leftover. The bottom of the barrel. Put a bag on her head and she'll do in a pinch." I was on a roll. Every passing comment I'd heard over the years in locker rooms and school halls bubbling out and spewing over this man that I'd made the embodiment of all my insecurities.

Because I liked him.

As I spiraled into a chasm of self-loathing and the

hateful words of others I'd faithfully absorbed and stored in my emotional walls over the years, I comforted myself with the fact that none of it was new. And nothing could make me feel worse than I already did.

"You think I came here last night for sex?"

I was wrong.

Despite Cian being the one who was hungover, I felt sickness curling in my gut. Of course he didn't want to fuck me. He wanted a friend. One of the boys.

He kept talking, but my mind was so much louder. The past flashing through my mind in a slideshow of shame and humiliation. I wrapped my arms around my stomach, willing the contents to stay put as I tried to find a way to surface, at least long enough to kick him out.

He didn't need to see me break.

"You need to go," I blurted, interrupting whatever he'd been saying. He cocked his head, hands half raised as though he wanted to touch me, but wasn't sure he would be welcome.

I sucked in a deep breath. Get him out, rebuild the walls. That was the plan.

"Our flight will be leaving soon, and I'm sure we don't need your teammates to catch you leaving my room at this time of the morning. Go and pack your bags. We can talk about this later."

His scowl was severe, but he couldn't argue with anything I'd just said.

With a look that told me he expected me to keep my word, he slipped out the door without further argument.

Now I just needed to avoid him for the rest of my life so he couldn't hurt me.

Easy.

CHAPTER
ELEVEN

Cian

BLAIR HAD SUCCESSFULLY AVOIDED me for two weeks.

After games, she disappeared before I could invite her out. When we traveled, she kept Dante between us like a shield. And she didn't answer the door to her hotel room when we were in Buffalo or Boston.

I'd messed up by turning up at her door drunk in Washington, but I didn't cope well when confronted by my childhood bully. Dylan Childs was born to be a defenseman. He was big, and mean, and had made my life hell when we were in the Junior League. My shoulder still occasionally ached from where he dislocated it in a 'friendly' game. Our coach drove me to the hospital and left me in the hands of medical staff who reset the shoulder and firmly told me to rest it for two months—no more hockey for the season. I'd nodded my ten-year-old head and promised to behave, then called my parents who were out of town for the day at a dog show. "You can walk home, can't you? It's your shoulder, not your legs. We'll see you at home. Ope, got to go. They're about to call Zeus's comp. Wish us luck!" I lied to the social worker and slipped out of the hospital without a backward glance. It wasn't the first time Dylan hurt me, and it wasn't the last time a dog was my parents' priority. I learned to adapt. When I got my scholarship to Fox, I thought I'd never see him again. I blossomed at Fox, making captain before senior year, and finding my people in my teammates.

It wasn't until my second year in professional hockey that I saw Dylan again. Despite the intervening years, no matter how many times I reminded myself that I was a fucking adult and didn't have to fear anyone, let alone the shitty kid who made my life hell, I still experienced a regression to the boy who was just trying to love the one thing he was good at.

None of that was Blair's fault, and I shouldn't have brought it to her doorstep, but apparently, drunk Cian doesn't give a shit about boundaries.

Maybe sober Cian didn't, either, because here I was, two days into our five-day break before the Global Series, taking the stairs to Blair's apartment two at a time.

I'd had time to think about what she said. The accusations she threw at me, and came to one glaring conclusion. We didn't know each other outside of work.

That, I could fix.

So here I was, knocking on Blair's door with the intention of taking her out for the day.

We could get to know each other outside of hockey, and I could casually drop into conversation that I wasn't the kind of guy who hooked up with puck bunnies.

And I could absolutely keep my mind from straying to how good it felt to wake up beside her. How her breast fit my palm perfectly, and her ass felt like heaven against my umm... yeah.

"I'm sorry, work has been crazy. I haven't had a chance to call you—Oh, it's you."

Her eyes were manga doll big behind her delicate gold-framed glasses, the toffee color glinting in the dim light of the hall. Her pajama pants hung low on her hips, a strip of soft skin visible below the hem of her T-shirt. I cast a quick look at my dick, mentally reminding it we weren't going to be invited to share her bed again anytime soon.

"Who were you expecting?" I asked, refocusing on why I had come.

"I've been ignoring my mother for the last week. She sent a text this morning that she would stop by today."

"So... how much do you want to keep avoiding her?" If this was my way in, I'd take it. We needed to keep building our relationship for the good of the club. Our social media manager couldn't indefinitely avoid a player. At least, that's what I told myself as I waited for her answer.

She narrowed her eyes at me, holding the door mostly closed while I stayed firmly on the corridor side of things.

"What do you have in mind?" she asked, her fingers flexing on the door as though she were considering slamming it in my face.

There were two ways I could play this.

I wanted to be the cool man of mystery who swept her off her feet for a surprise day of fun and bonding, but the reality was that she didn't trust me, and I had a suspicion that she and I weren't on the same page with a lot of things. So instead of forcing my way in and insisting she get dressed, I laid my cards on the table.

"I volunteer at an animal shelter on weekends when I'm at home. I'm heading in today, and thought you might like to join me. You get unlimited puppy cuddles and can hand feed the bunnies. There's a cat called Garfield who is the embodiment of the cartoon. He has a death stare that scares the dogs from twenty yards away."

Her eyes searched mine, fingers still gripping her door hard. What could I do to convince her? Perhaps that was the problem. I couldn't make the decision for her, and trying to push seemed to make her leave faster.

I tucked my hands into my pockets and let her look. No secrets here, just someone who really wanted to spend the day with this uber defensive, but surprisingly interesting person.

A curl dropped over her eye, and she blew it away, raking her hand through her hair for good measure.

"Give me a couple of minutes to get dressed, and we'll go."

She slammed the door, only to open it a second later.

"You'd better wait in here. Just in case my mother does show up and we have to jump out the window."

"We're on the third floor."

"You underestimate my desire to avoid my family."

I chuckled at what I really hoped was a joke and stepped inside, closing the door behind me while she ran for her bedroom.

Little had changed since I was last in the space, but with our schedule, and the hours I knew she pulled, it wasn't unexpected. There was a small collection of cups and glasses on her coffee table and a pile of clothing over the back of a dining chair.

The kitchen was relatively clean, though there were a couple of takeout containers by the trash can. I wondered what she would think of my obsessively neat space.

Wandering to the entry and back, I checked the door I assumed was Blair's bedroom.

Still closed.

I strolled a circle of her living room, smiling at the picture from her hockey days and ended up back in the kitchen. Back to the coffee table, though this time I loaded up on the glasses and brought them with me back to the sink. Next time around, I retrieved the coffee mugs.

When Blair reappeared a little while later, I was elbow deep in dish soap, scrubbing dried queso off a plate.

"What are you doing?"

I whipped around and tried for a casual lean, cursing as I drenched my shirt.

"Ready to go?"

I could play this off, even if the pile of unfolded laundry haunted me for the rest of the day.

Grabbing the nearest dishtowel, I dried my hands and took in her outfit. A cute little T-shirt with a turtle print and "this is how I roll" stretched across her chest in a way I wasn't at all noticing. There was a pink blush to her cheeks and lips that could have been makeup, and best of all, she was wearing my favorite jeans. The ones that cupped her ass perfectly.

I'd never considered myself an ass guy, but that seemed to be changing in Blair's presence.

"You washed my dishes," she said, ignoring my encouragement to get going.

"I have a short attention span. Idle hands and all that. Come on, my truck's outside."

She stared at me a moment longer before reluctantly allowing me to steer her out the front door.

"It's weird to wash someone else's dishes. You get that, right?" she asked as we belted in, and I started the engine.

"I do it at Oscar and Mia's place all the time."

She shook her head, staring out the window as we pulled away from the curb.

"It's not far from here. The shelter, that is."

My hands stuck to the steering wheel as I navigated us the couple of blocks to our destination. I'd downplayed the significance of this shelter. No one knew I came here.

Not Mack. Not Oscar. No one.

I had such a complicated relationship with my parents, and animals had always felt like the catalyst.

No time for a son, there were dogs to train.

But the truth was, I loved animals. I'd have adopted half the shelter years ago if it wasn't unfair when I traveled so much.

Coming here gave me the connection without complication. Without the reminder of my parents.

We parked at the back of the lot, under a tree, and hustled toward the shelter. I shivered in the brisk breeze, regretting not taking the chance to change into a dry shirt. The shelter was always warm, and the work was often dirty so we'd be fine inside. Though my shirt probably wouldn't last the day. As the door chimed, announcing our entrance, Katie looked up from behind the desk with a welcoming smile in place. The expression warmed into something less practiced when she recognized me.

"Cian! Welcome back." I grinned and held my knuckles out for a pound as the teen bounced out of her seat. "Decided to grace us with your presence today. You know Girtie has been missing you."

The ring-necked parrot was a long-time resident of the shelter, and a menace to the volunteers who passed too close to her cage. I had a chunk missing from my left ear that I'd passed off as an old hockey injury.

It was Girtie-induced.

I rolled my eyes at her and held a hand back for Blair, making quick work of introduction.

"She's going to help out today, so make sure you give her the good ones so I don't look bad."

"They're all good ones," Katie said, grinning at me, then turning her smile on Blair.

"Come on through. We have some spare rubber boots you can put on, if you want to save your sneakers."

Once we had appropriate footwear, Katie led us back to the exercise area.

Unlike other shelters in the area, this branch of Austin Animal Allies was set up more like a pet motel than a shelter. As animals came in off the street, they were assessed for social skills and trauma, alongside their physical condition, and were accommodated in different areas dependent on temperament. The ones who were well socialized were given yard time every day to burn off excess energy and ensure their well-being, playing with others of a similar size in a space full of enrichment toys and a shallow pool for wading. This was where I wanted Blair to spend the day, tossing a ball and enjoying the energy of dogs likely to be reclaimed by loving families within days of entry to the shelter.

I scratched the ear of a cocker spaniel I hadn't met before and offered a tennis ball to Blair. I gestured toward a bulldog who was already dancing in place, his eyes fixated on her hand.

"Toss it as hard as you can. Bruce loves the chase, even if he'll only bring it back once or twice before he needs a rest."

She glanced at me quickly, then hauled off and threw as

hard as she could. Bruce took chase with a grunting wheeze that had the same cadence as a steam train.

"Oh, my God. He's adorable."

"He's a machine, all right. Just don't leave him alone with peanut butter treats."

She laughed, and the sound echoed through my chest, carefree and happy.

I wanted to stay and bask in the joy radiating out of her as she bent to say hello to a three-legged labrador who was another resident I hadn't met, but there was something I needed to do first.

"I'll be back in a few, okay? Just chill here and I'll come find you when I'm done."

Her agreement was lost in a shriek as the lab decided to cement their friendship with a kiss.

Chuckling, I closed the gate behind me and headed for the less-pretty part of the shelter. As I entered a hall lined with bolted wire doors, I called a greeting to Dan, the maintenance manager of the shelter.

"How's my girl today?" I asked, stopping in front of the second to last door in the row.

"Pretty much the same. I don't think she's let anyone get close since you started the season."

I sighed as Dan turned his attention back to the light globe he was replacing.

Before I entered the cage, I took a moment to shake out my shirt, allowing my scent to waft through the small space. In the back corner, a black nose rose out of a bundle of blankets.

"How are you today, my pretty girl?" I asked in a low voice, sinking onto my haunches. A black ear cocked, but otherwise there was no response.

With slow movements, I eased the gate open and

slipped inside, keeping my eyes on the wall as I sat side-on to the wary animal.

"I heard you haven't been very nice to the people who feed you, baby girl. What has you feeling unsafe?" I asked, keeping my voice low and soothing.

A whippy tail twitched, and I smothered a smile as I continued to speak to the wall, easing my body a half inch closer to the back of the cage.

It always went like this.

For the first month, the rottweiler had been vicious, attacking anyone who approached her cage. It had taken time and consistency for her to trust me in her space, and last time I'd been here, she had allowed Dan in to clean her kennel without needing a muzzle and a sedative. I was determined to make her like me. We'd been close a couple of times, she'd come as far as to sniff my knuckles before retreating to her nest, but the day she trusted me enough to pet her, I'd feel unstoppable.

"We won our last game in Chicago," I told her, easing a little closer. "I think we're in for a shot at the cup this year. But don't tell anyone I said that, or they'll call me a jinx."

I kept up a constant babble, eyes focused away from her corner so she didn't feel trapped, and after long enough for my ass to go numb, a miracle happened.

I'd shuffled over halfway through the room, head turned away and hand resting on the floor closer to the nest of bedding when a soft wetness brushed against my knuckles. I paused in the middle of explaining the difference between a slap shot and a wrist shot. Shaking off the shock, I returned to my description of stick handling and cast a quick glance beside me. Seelie, the rottweiler who had caught my heart the first time I'd seen her trembling in fear, had stretched her beautiful body across the floor, her nose barely touching my knuckles as she watched me with cautious eyes. Her flanks showed scarring from a history I didn't want to think about, silver gouges in her fur telling the story of human cruelty. Yet here she was, giving her trust to me.

"You're such a good girl," I whispered to her, keeping completely still as she eased a little closer, rubbing her muzzle more firmly against my knuckles. My vision blurred, and I couldn't have given less of a shit. This beautiful survivor was showing me a level of trust I'd never expected to earn.

And that was before she pulled herself up and crawled over my lap.

"Seelie." My voice broke on the word. I wanted to stroke her. To show her how I cared for her, but I knew this moment could break in an instant. She was testing me. Seeing if I would act out the same way others had toward her.

I had to be patient and prove myself worthy.

And in that moment, my thoughts went, inexplicably, to Blair.

CHAPTER
TWELVE

Blair

THE BULLDOG WAS SNORING at my feet, and my hands were crusted with dirt from patting so many different dogs. I was tired from throwing ball, yet energized in a way I hadn't been in a long time. It had been hours since my last coffee, and I wasn't even missing the caffeine fix.

I was, however, missing Cian.

He'd told me he would return, but as time rolled on, I wasn't sure whether he'd forgotten me. Or found someone else.

Stop it. Positive vibes only while we're here.

I wandered out of the gate, locking it behind me, and along the corridor I'd seen him walk down earlier.

I took a couple of turns, hoping I could find my way to the front to ask for help, when Katie found me.

"Have you seen Cian?"

The girl blinked at me a couple of times.

"He's probably with Seelie."

Seelie. Right.

She blinked at me again before seeming to realize I had no idea who she was talking about.

"Take that corridor there, then first left, then right at the end, then go all the way to the back, second to last cage."

It was my turn to blink, but the girl was already gone.

Luckily, the directions were rather self-explanatory as I moved down a corridor lined with cages and heard a soft murmuring coming from the back.

Cian was seated in the middle of a cage with a huge black and tan dog stretched out across his knee. A tear streaked down his face as he spoke about... puck handling?

The dog was a beast, scarred and muscled, with a missing ear and a warped lip, but he spoke to it like it was a baby.

"You're such a good girl. Do you want to hear more about our season stats? Maybe I can teach you how to wrap your stick properly."

"Cian?" It felt wrong to interrupt this moment, and as the dog's head swung up, her low growl made me wish I'd kept my mouth shut.

"Seelie," he admonished gently, smoothing a hand down her flank with a look of wonder as he followed the movement with his eyes.

The dog swung its head around to look him in the eye before letting out a chuff and lowering her head back to her paws.

"She finally trusts me," he breathed.

I dropped into a crisscross position on the floor and watched as Cian spent a few more moments stroking the beast before reaching into his pocket to retrieve a treat for her. She took it with a mouth far more gentle than I would have expected and seemed to know it was her cue to move. With a big sigh, she heaved her body off the man who tamed her and curled up in a pile of blankets against the far wall.

Cian used the wall at his back to pull himself up, wincing as he worked the blood back into his legs. I wondered how long she had been lying across his legs, especially as I held the gate open for him and he hobbled out, locking up behind him.

His eyes were dazed as we wandered toward the front of the shelter in silence.

"All finished?" Katie asked as we swapped our boots out for sneakers and headed for the front door.

"Yeah, we are. Sorry we didn't help with the cleaning. I'll come in before we fly out to lend a hand."

He didn't mention Seelie, and the omission made me feel like I'd had the opportunity to witness something private. Something special.

"Sorry I left you for so long. I guess I lost track of time," he said as we headed toward his truck.

"It's okay, it seems like you were doing something important."

For once, I didn't mean the observation as a barb. It wasn't a jealous attack. I was genuinely glad he'd been able to form a bond with an animal that so clearly needed the love.

"Are you going to adopt her?" I asked, stretching my seat belt across my chest.

He grunted, starting the engine and easing the truck out from beneath the overhang.

"I'd love to, but I don't think it's fair to her with my schedule the way it is now. I couldn't exactly ask someone to dog sit a traumatized rottweiler while I fly across the country."

He had a point, but the thought of her staying in that small cage alone made my eyes water.

"Are you hungry?" Cian asked suddenly, like he was shaking off the untenable situation.

My stomach let out a growl, answering for me and making Cian laugh.

"There's a dope burger place a couple of blocks from here. The waffle fries are next level."

I'd seen a side to Cian today that I didn't want to acknowledge existed. His vulnerability was crumbling my own defenses in a way I couldn't allow.

But a burger couldn't hurt. Right?

"Why not," I said, not quite able to bring myself to fully agree.

Cian shot me a smile and put his turn signal on, smoothly sliding around the corner and onto a quieter street.

"It's not a flashy place, but the food is amazing and the chance of us being recognized is small."

The good thing about living in Texas was that hockey wasn't the first sport that came to mind. Basketball? Rodeo? Football? Hell yes. Frozen rinks and ice skates? Not so much. The Aces fanbase was rabid, but to an everyday Texan, they were just big guys who didn't care about throwing a pig skin.

After a couple more turns, he pulled up in front of a diner that looked like it had stood since the fifties. The faded turquoise bricks were coated in dust, and the neon sign had a busted globe.

"Trust me," he said as he held his hands up, offering

assistance in climbing down from the passenger seat. I could do it myself, already had at the shelter, but instead of making a fuss, I leaned out of the doorway and put my hands on his shoulders. His hands wrapped around my ribs, and I willed my heart to settle as he slowly lowered me to the ground. We stood toe to toe, neither of us dropping our grip on the other, and I licked my lips. His eyes darted down to track the movement.

Step away, Blair.

Instead, I tempted fate and tilted my head back. His head dipped a little closer in response, and my eyes fluttered closed as his breath coasted over my lips.

Bang!

We jolted apart, Cian pushing me behind him as he whirled toward the threat... which turned out to be an old truck backfiring as it turned out of the parking lot across the street.

As the rusted bulk trundled toward the intersection, I slipped out from under Cian's protective arm and strode toward the diner's entrance.

What the fuck am I doing?

I knew better than this. No matter what he had said in Washington, the evidence was clear. Whenever puck bunnies entered the room, Blair disappeared. It was a foundational rule of the universe, and something I'd seen time and time again, since the very first moment we met.

Not good enough.

Pretty enough.

Enough.

I pulled my walls around me like a protective coat as I slid into a booth and ordered a ginger ale.

Cian ordered the same and added a cheeseburger and waffle fries. I asked her to double it, and he grinned at me as the waitress pocketed her order pad and headed toward the kitchen.

"We have the same order," he said, linking his fingers on top of the table.

"It's a pretty standard order."

He hummed noncommittally and sat back in his seat, watching me closely.

"If you could be one character from a video game, who would you be?" he asked.

"Bowser. You?"

His eyebrows disappeared behind his ridiculously perfect bangs.

"Bowser? Come on. You have to elaborate."

"Nuh-uh. That's not the game. Now, come on. It's your turn."

"Well... if you're going to be Bowser, I guess that makes me Princess Peach."

"What?" I shrieked, smothering my giggles with a palm as the nearby diners turned to see what the fuss was.

"Why the hell would you be Peach?"

His eyes sparkled. "It seems only fair."

"That..." I gave up, sitting back with a huff when I realized he'd hold to the rules just the same as I did.

"Fine. If you could only eat one protein for the rest of your life, what would you choose?"

"Nuts." I glanced at him in surprise. Surely an athlete like him would be a red meat kind of guy.

"They're more versatile. Plus, I wouldn't have to give up peanut butter cups."

I shook my head, sitting back and thanking the waitress as she placed our drinks in front of us. Cian took a long sip, watching me as I fiddled with my straw.

"So? What's your protein?"

"Fish."

"You are just full of surprises."

"I could live on sushi, if I had to."

He nodded, holding his hands out as though writing in a book.

"Noted. Next time, sushi."

A small thrill ran through me at the mention of a next time, but I squashed it down. This couldn't happen again if I wanted to maintain a professional distance. Cian O'Leary's friendship was a path more dangerous than any Temple of Doom or booby-trapped pyramid. It was only a matter of time before I found myself at the bottom of a pit or crushed beneath a careless boulder.

Maybe I shouldn't have sat up late watching old Indiana Jones movies, I decided as Cian sipped on his drink.

"Favorite age so far?" he said.

That was a hard one. I'd loved my time playing hockey, but that had been while I was still at home and dealing with my mother and sister daily. I shuddered. Definitely not then.

College was okay, though I never really felt like I fit in, and while I loved what I did now, sometimes the loneliness dragged me down.

"Twenty-four," I decided, lifting my soda in a toast and taking a long sip.

"Aren't you twenty-three?"

I shrugged, the edge of my lips twitching.

"Call me an optimist."

"The best is yet to come?" He lifted a brow in challenge, and I let the smile free.

We were interrupted from our game briefly as our burgers and fries arrived, and I reluctantly agreed they were the best I'd had in Austin. Conversation flowed easily, and before I knew it, the light was fading in the sky.

"I think you might have missed your mother's visit," Cian mused, stretching his shoulders. His shirt rode up over his abdomen, revealing a pale stripe of skin I wished I were brave enough to lick.

"Are you ready to go home?"

He slid out of the booth and held out a hand to me. Instead of accepting the offer, I shuffled out by myself and headed for the exit as he tapped his phone to pay at the counter. I was well fed and had had a wonderful time with a man who was funny, charming, and attentive.

The freakout had begun.

Cian tried to engage me in conversation as he steered us toward my apartment, but my mind was filled with slideshows of boys from my past who I thought I could trust. Of sneering rejections and laughing ridicule. At the center of it all was my sister telling me I should have known better.

That no one loves an ugly duckling.

I dove out of the truck as we rolled to a stop outside my apartment, almost rolling an ankle in my haste to get away.

"Wait. Blair, wait!" he called, jumping out after me. His truck continued to rumble, and I wondered if he'd thought to pull the parking brake.

"Thanks for the day. I had a great time. See you," I rushed out, all but sprinting for the door to my building.

"Wait, what's wrong?" He caught my elbow, pulling me around to face him.

"I thought we had fun today."

"Fun. Sure," I spat, thankful that the parking lot was quiet and no one was likely to hear our confrontation.

"What did I do wrong? I thought we were friends, but

you're acting like I broke your favorite laptop and spit in your coffee."

"What's the catch?" I asked, the challenge clear in my tone. If he wanted to do this, I would. Cards on the table. It seemed like a good enough night to have my heart broken.

"What do you mean?"

"My first kiss was Bobby Findlay. I found out later it was on a dare, and he had tried to swap with a kid who had to lick a toilet."

Words were coming out of my mouth, and I wished they wouldn't. But the memories that were screaming through my head on the drive home had decided this man should bear witness.

"The man I lost my virginity to won fifty dollars on a bet. The longest relationship I ever had was a secret because the guy didn't want his friends knowing who he spent time with. You say you want to be friends, and so I'm asking you. What do you get out of it?"

He dragged a hand across his mouth, not quite covering his sneer as I stood my ground and dared him to tell me the truth.

There had to be something. The fact that he didn't find me attractive wasn't the wakeup call he thought it was and I'd grown tired of the back and forth. He would give me the truth whether he wanted to or not. No more head games.

"Fuck it," he growled, grasping the back of my neck with one large hand and tugging hard. Our bodies crashed together, his mouth covering mine before I could voice a word of protest.

This... was unexpected. His tongue ran along the seam of my mouth, not so much asking as demanding to be let in. I surrendered before I knew what was happening, and could only feel as he licked into my mouth with wicked lashes that dampened my panties and weakened my knees. His arm wrapped around my waist, holding me tight against the erection that strained at his jeans.

Feeling overwhelmed by the experience of *him*, I dug my fingers into his chest, trying to ground myself in the rush of arousal that coursed through me.

At that moment, a vision of Georgia, the pretty sister, Mom's favorite, popped in my head and gave me the strength to push away from the man who made me weak.

Breathing hard, I wiped my mouth with the back of my hand, keeping my eyes on his face so they didn't drop to the biological response that every man had when they were close to getting some pussy.

"Do you remember the first time we met?"

He was breathing as hard as I was, eyes unfocused as he tried to translate the question I'd asked.

"Umm." He dragged a hand through his hair. "At training camp? Three years ago. You asked us to run a drill all over again because you'd dropped your coffee and missed the shot." His smile made a reappearance, as though it were a fond memory.

The hate and vitriol I'd caught from a couple of the players as they headed for the locker rooms had been a quick lesson in timing and priorities.

I shook my head, because regardless of how we remembered that particular day, the answer was wrong anyway.

"Five years ago."

He cocked his head, clearly confused, and I huffed a mirthless laugh.

Forgettable.

Replaceable.

Nothing.

Five years ago

When I grew up, *I wanted to own a sports bar. I perched on a stool at the bar and ordered a soda while the Wildcats took on the Blizzards on the TV. The Wildcats were looking strong, but as the Blizzards set up for a power play, a closeup of the Wildcats goalie showed him chewing hard on his mouthguard with a hard look in his eye.*

"Do you think they'll make it?" I jumped at the male voice, so close to my ear, and swiveled around to face a pair of stunning olive eyes.

"Their goalie's nervous," I said, nodding at the screen as the wingers passed the puck between themselves.

It took the players two minutes before they scored in the five hole.

"Krishnoff is slowing down. I heard a rumor this is his last year," the guy said, leaning his elbows against the bar a little closer than was polite. He was handsome, with dark hair and darker lashes framing those eyes. He was built like an athlete, and I wondered what sport he played. At a table in the corner, guys of a similar build were decked out in the black, orange, and white of Fox U. Not surprising. You couldn't go anywhere in this college town without running into students from the academy.

A disturbance in the air made a chill run up the back of my neck, and the men seemed to feel it too as they turned toward the door and watched the new arrival.

Dressed in an outfit completely inappropriate both for the setting and the time of year, a redheaded bombshell strutted in, wearing four-inch stilettos that would have made me face-plant if I even looked at them wrong.

Georgia Kennedy, who went by Gia—because of course she did—was destined to be an actress. Everyone who knew her knew this as fact. What not as many people knew was that she was my private nightmare. She had been the instigator of pranks, cruel jokes, and all the most humiliating moments of my life to date.

She strode toward my bar mate like she was on a mission.

And just like that, it was time for this five on a good day to make way for my sister.

I slid from the stool quietly and left my almost friend to his happily ever after... for the night.

Gia would be hunting for any scrap of acceptance to crush beneath her perfect feet the second I came by it again.

CHAPTER
THIRTEEN

Cian

"So you see?" she demanded, waving her arms around while I wracked my brain for the night in question. Who the hell remembered a chance encounter from five years ago? I knew for a fact I wouldn't have touched her sister because even back then I'd been more interested in keeping my team in line than picking up, but suddenly things were falling into place in a way I really didn't enjoy. The disappearances every time we went out. The inexplicable frostiness despite my best attempts to be nice to her.

The fact that this realization came on the heels of an intense attraction I'd developed to who she was as a person fueled my own temper.

"What am I supposed to see, Blair? I'm sorry that you've had to put up with assholes in your past, but I'm not the guy you're making me out to be."

I shouldn't have found it adorable the way she puffed herself up, her hair adding to the pissed off chipmunk look she was sporting. She had made an assumption about me that was really fucking wrong, and that alone seemed to be her reason for pushing me away.

"You're just wasting time with me until someone better comes along. You know it, and I know it, so why don't you save both of us some time and leave me the hell alone." She stomped her sneaker to prove her point, but I was beyond done listening to the bullshit she was telling herself.

"Can you stop assuming you know what I'm thinking? If you want to know, ask me. Because I'm getting really fucking tired of being cast as the bad guy. I like you. I really do. I'm sorry if you don't, but that's on you."

Her jaw dropped, fists balling at her sides, but it was my time to talk and she was damn well going to hear it.

"I bought into your company line for a long time. You're 'one of the boys', 'the bland girl', but you know what? You're more than that. You're fucking gorgeous, you're funny, caring, and someone I really want to spend more time with. So I think it's you who needs to decide. Are you ready to take a chance on someone? Or are you going to stay behind those walls of self-hatred and let your fucking mother win."

Shit. Why the hell did I bring up her mother? You never get in the way of family feuds.

"I think you need to go." Her body deflated so fast, I had to hold myself in place to keep from trying to catch her wilted body. I'd spent so much of the morning being patient and kind with one hurt female, only to cast the final arrow at another.

Maybe I was the asshole she accused me of being.

With a tight nod, I forced myself back to the truck, which still idled in the parking lot, doors open and diesel fumes sweetening the air.

Don't look at her. Don't look at her.

Her face was ruined. Features cast in a sallow light, as though I'd pulled her spirit out with my words.

Did I regret them? No. But perhaps it would have been more productive coming from Mia... or a licensed professional. If we were closer to Chicago, I could recommend my cousin's wife but...

I cut off the mental detour and buckled my belt. I'd caused her enough stress for one day. Time to go home and come up with a new plan of action to win her over.

If it was still possible.

Thirteen minutes and forty-two seconds later, I let myself into Mia and Oscar's house and interrupted their dinner.

"You didn't say that," Mia chided as I dropped my head to the table and Oscar placed an open beer next to me.

"I did. I don't know why... I couldn't stop the words. Will you scratch my head again?"

A much larger than expected palm landed on my head.

"Her head scratches are for me only."

I snorted. "Okay, Caveman."

I didn't care who did it; I just needed some form of physical affection while I royally blew up my life. Oscar moved his hand over my head a few times before there was a sigh and a much smaller hand took its place.

"Thank you for your pity," I mumbled into the table, resisting the urge to purr under Mia's blunt nails.

"So what's your next move? Are you finally leaving her alone? Or going all out stalker?" Oscar asked, his chair squeaking as he settled back.

"I'm pretty sure I can find a happy medium between those two options, but I need help. You're not helping me."

"I don't know if there's anything to do right now," Mia

said gently, keeping up the stroking like it would soften her delivery. "It sounds like Blair has some work to do, and while you've done a good job of bringing her awareness to it—" Oscar snorted. "While you've done a good job bringing her awareness to it, it's up to her to decide whether she is ready to work through it or not. You can't do it for her."

My friends were the worst helpers in the history of the world.

"So you're saying to give up on her?"

"I'm saying that she has to do some work on herself. That doesn't mean you give up on her, but it does mean you give her space. In the meantime, maybe I could have a word with her. See if she needs a friendly ear."

My friends were the best helpers in the world.

"Yes. Please. Talk to her. You can tell her I'm a good guy and fix everything."

Mia held up her hands like she was at gunpoint. "I'm not making any promises."

"Thank you, thank you, thank you. Oscar, kiss your wife for me."

"I'll kiss her for myself," he growled as he skirted the table and pulled her into an inappropriate kiss.

"Y'know, if I wasn't used to it, this could be really uncomfortable right now," I muttered, finally feeling settled enough to swig my beer.

"Weren't you leaving?" Oscar asked as his hands roamed down Mia's back, cupping her ass possessively.

"Yup, definitely. Thank you, Mia, for the offer. I wholeheartedly accept. For the love of God, wait until you hear the front door close before you start stripping off. See you later."

I wasted no time vacating my best friend's house, and

still caught the first moan as I slammed the door firmly behind me.

I was going to find a stuffed pigeon and leave it in his locker for that.

But maybe after Mia helped with my love life...

FOURTEEN

Blair

THE TRAINING CENTER was quiet for once, players choosing workout times on their own schedule during the week before the global series. Many of the staff chose to work from home as they coordinated the logistics of sending a hockey team overseas for two days. I'd already drafted up themed posts for most of the guys heading over to Helsinki, but the walls of my apartment had been closing in on me, and I found the coldness of the rink comforting when my mind felt ready to burn out.

I had revisited Cian's speech so many times in my head, it felt like some demonic spell that would open a rift in the earth for me to fall down.

"I come in peace." The gentle feminine voice was a surprise. Oscar Cavanaugh's wife, Mia, was stunningly gorgeous, even in a sweater and jeans. Her dark hair was swept up in a simple ponytail, and I felt a moment of envy for how straight and silky it looked as it swung behind her.

"What are you doing here?"

"I brought coffee. Want some?" She held out a cup displaying the Wild Brew logo on the side.

"I asked the barista what your order was," she admitted, her cheeks coloring a soft pink.

"Why does this feel like a bribe?"

"Because it sort of is?" She dropped into the seat beside me, turning her body to face me.

"I may be a trained therapist, but I'm also from a fucked-up family. I specialize in that shit. So I'm here as a friend, asking if you'd like to talk."

Her features were relaxed, no signs of deceit, or any hint she was fishing for information to use against me. That didn't mean...

"Cian sent you."

"I offered."

"Why?"

Mia sighed and picked at the lid of her own coffee. Down on the practice rink, the Zamboni roared to life as the maintenance crew re-leveled the ice.

"I don't have a lot of friends. Oscar is the extrovert out of the two of us. Similar to Cian." She shot me a quick look. "When Oscar first came into my life, I thought I was broken beyond repair. I just didn't believe anyone could or should love me. Oscar was... well... you've met him. He doesn't really understand the word no, unless you're talking consent. Anyway, I almost let my insecurities destroy the best thing that ever happened to me. Cian was one of the people who helped me believe I deserved this life Oscar and I have built together. So why did I volunteer to come? I guess I'm passing on the good karma. I would like to get to know you, because you seem like someone worth knowing. And I'm not just saying that for Cian's sake. You guys have to work out your stuff between you. But if you ever want to talk, I'm here." She glanced up and away again, then stood, clapping her hands.

"I'm sure you are incredibly busy, so I'll let you get back to it. Oscar can give you my number if you ever want to use it." Her small smile told me she hoped I would.

"Thank you," I choked out as she turned to walk away.

"We all need someone, Blair. Life is pretty dull when we hide behind our walls all alone." With another nod, she strode down the aisle of chairs and headed for the exit.

I turned back to my computer to find the screen had gone black, and when I glanced up, Mia was gone.

Feeling like some *Touched by an Angel* shit had just gone down, I packed up my belongings and headed for Dante's office. She'd had a couple of small PR issues come up and had promised to walk me through how she'd handled them.

"How's your day going?" she asked as I stepped into her perfectly appointed office. I'd never done much with my own space because I preferred to sit in the stands, closer to the action and the players in case I needed to talk to them while I worked. Dante's office looked like an upscale law firm that would make grown men cry if they didn't fall in line.

"A little weird but productive. How's yours?"

With pleasantries exchanged, we settled in and got to work, running through the media plan, and how she instructed the players to proceed in each of the cases she'd handled.

As we were wrapping up the final case study, she paused, an odd look on her face.

"Can I ask you something that might be a little personal?"

Dante was straight forward, ball busting, and exactly who you wanted when shit hit the fan.

She rarely asked permission, and as long as I'd known her, we'd never spoken about personal things.

"Sure. Shoot."

"Is something going on between you and O'Leary?"

Her face was carefully blank, giving nothing away.

"What makes you think that?" I asked in lieu of an answer. What could I say? He might like me, or he could be setting up to break me.

"He spent the night in your hotel room in Washington."

I hid my surprise, wondering why she was bringing it up now.

"Nothing happened." I could have explained the situation more, but it felt like a betrayal to tell her he was wasted and vulnerable. The team had a strict code of behavior for away games, and getting pass-out drunk was definitely a no-no.

"You were photographed leaving a diner together two days ago."

Why would I have been...? Right. I wouldn't. But Cian would.

"We went for lunch after doing some volunteer work. We're... friends." I almost choked on the word.

Dante nodded, keen eyes studying me like I was another problem to solve. Maybe I was.

"Take the rest of the day off. Keep off social media, and when the *nothing* turns into *something*, for the love of God, let me know first. Okay?"

"You really think someone like him would look twice at someone like me?" I asked, voicing the heart of my insecurity. He was too pretty. Too talented. Too... him. Why was he focused on me?

She sighed. "He'd be lucky to have you, Blair. Take it from someone who has already failed at the marriage thing. Compatibility is critical in a relationship, and it has nothing to do with looks. It has everything to do with how they make you feel. O'Leary looks for you when he enters the room. I've seen it. So whatever's going on, decide how you feel about it. Make your decision, or don't, but have all the information."

Her lips quirked in an empathic smile before she clapped her hands and stood. With firm strokes, she brushed down her jacket, as though straightening herself out of the emotional moment.

"I'm thinking of finding a therapist," I blurted. The idea was as much of a surprise to me as it was to her. But I'd heard one too many people I respected tell me very similar things over the last couple of days. If I wanted to get out of my own way, and maybe find a way to be happy, I had some work to do.

"I think that's a wonderful idea."

"It won't affect my work."

"I know."

I picked at my nail, wondering if I should say the next part.

"I like him. Cian."

She huffed a laugh and squeezed my arm on her way to the door.

"I know."

"Is there anything you don't know?" I asked.

She paused in the doorway, one heel raised. Her bloodred fingernail tapped against the wooden frame.

"Whether spring will arrive early this year. I'm no groundhog."

I laughed as Dante strutted her Pennsylvanian ass out of the office, leaving me to my thoughts.

Nope. Not doing that.

Regardless of what Dante told me, I had work to do.

A quick side quest to the Wild Bean, and a short drive later, I pulled into the parking lot of my building and found a familiar truck parked in my usual spot.

I gathered my caffeine and my courage and found Cian sitting on the front stoop of my building.

"I thought you were ignoring me again, but you were at the training center," he said by way of greeting.

"Mia found me there just fine."

He sighed and stood with a wince. "Of course she did. She refused to give me an update. Said I could come grovel under my own steam."

I stepped around him to unlock the entry, briefly considering shutting the door in his face, but it was time to be an adult and not let the intrusive thoughts win.

"So you're here to grovel?" I asked, holding the door wide as he retrieved a takeout bag from the step he'd been sitting on.

"Apology sushi?"

"Come up."

His footsteps were loud in the quiet of the stairwell as we made our way up to my apartment. He stood patiently as I opened the door, and waited for me to wave him inside. For someone who kept turning up in my life, he certainly acted like he had manners.

Heading straight for the kitchen, he cleared a space on the counter and began to unpack an unholy amount of sushi.

"Were you expecting your whole team to show up here?"

"I was expecting you to be in a worse mood, honestly. It's always better to be overprepared."

"Were you planning on standing in the hall and tossing nori rolls at me until I calmed down?"

He snorted, flicking his gaze up to mine before returning to his unpacking.

"Something like that."

He moved around my kitchen like he belonged there. The illusion was broken only when he had to ask which cupboard held glasses and which dishes.

"So..." he said as we sat on the sofa with our food. "Have you been on social media today?"

His tone was curious, but he perched on the edge of his seat, body tense.

"No... actually, Dante told me to stay off it."

Now he sat back, stretching his arm along the back of the sofa and crossing his ankles in front of him.

"Good. That's good. How's your sushi?"

I took a big bite and gave him a rice filled grin.

What could be trending that they didn't want me to see? The only answers I could come up with were either a worldwide coffee shortage, or... me.

While Cian worked his chopsticks like a pro, picking up pieces of nigiri and popping them in his mouth like we were in an authentic restaurant, I slid my phone out of my pocket and fired up my social media page. The first photo on the feed was of Cian and me, but before I could read any comments, my phone disappeared from my hand.

"Nope. You do not need to read that."

"Cian." I held my hand out, giving him my best *don't fuck with me* face.

"Sorry, babe. I'm doing this for your own good."

"Weren't you mad at me, like, yesterday? You should be happy that karma is coming for me."

The scowl he turned on me was the same expression he wore when he first hit the ice for a game he didn't know whether they would win. Determination to beat the odds.

"Never. I was mad you don't trust me to tell you the truth. Doesn't mean you need to read the inside thoughts these trolls thought everyone should have access to."

So I was right. Someone, somewhere had caught us on our day out and decided to let the world know we don't belong together. Like I couldn't have told them that.

"Give me the phone. It's better to deal with these things head-on."

He stretched his arm a little further from me. "Nuh-uh. Dante told you to stay off it. I'm helping."

"Cian." I grabbed his arm, trying to pull his hand close enough to get my cell back. God, he was strong. Those muscles didn't move an inch as I kneeled up and tried to find more leverage.

Nope.

Well, if I couldn't bring it to me, I'd go to it. I crawled across his lap as I caught a hold on his hand and tried to pry the device from his fingers.

"Even your freaking fingers are strong! How?!"

Cian choked out a strangled laugh. The noise pulled me from my quest and I realized the position I'd put myself in. My breasts were all but pressed into his face as I'd stretched for his hand. My knees were on either side of his hips and beneath me he was hard.

"Oops," I muttered, sitting back so we were almost nose to nose.

"I don't mind." His smile was tight.

"Please give me my phone."

Those beautiful olive eyes flicked over my face, assessing. He really did think he was protecting me from whatever comments were on the photo. The fact was I was a big girl, and I had to be able to read criticism and not react to it if I wanted to continue to work in this field. If I took over from Dante at the end of the season, would I be able to help athletes if I was worried some internet troll was going to hurt my feelings?

Slowly, his arm dropped. His lips screwed tight as he handed the device to me, but when I made a move to get off him, he gripped my thighs in those ridiculously strong hands.

"If you're reading that shit, you're not going anywhere."

I gave him a look that I hope he interpreted as *you're being ridiculous* and reopened the page.

Beauty and the beast. The delicious Cian O'Leary out with some dog in downtown Austin.

The picture was of us beside his truck, standing a lot closer together than I noticed at the time.

The comments section was vicious.

@olearysfuturebeau - maybe he's doing some kind of make a wish for the terminally ugly

@hockey_fan23 - Beauty and the beast, lol. Definitely a butterface.

@puckbunny4lyf - No, hear me out. She's auditioning for the dour wife so he can go out and f**k bunnies without the bad PR

@aces4thechampionship - O'Leary! Blink twice if you need help!

The comments went on and on. Variations of the same theme. Too ugly for a hockey player. Maybe he has weird kinks and she has a beard. Maybe he's being held hostage.

Some were so absurd they were funny.

"I don't give a fuck what they say, but it matters if it screws up any remaining chance I had with you."

I tossed my phone on the coffee table behind me.

"I couldn't care less what a bunch of keyboard warriors have to say about me. I tell myself worse things every day. That's child's play." I waved my hand in the direction of my phone and shrugged.

"That makes me really sad."

"What?"

His grip tightened on my thighs, then he rubbed his palms over them, like he needed to know I was solid on top of him.

"I hate the thought of you being mean to yourself. Let alone worse than the shit those assholes said. You're the only one I would have wanted to share that day with, so fuck anyone who says different."

I shifted in his lap, caught between discomfort at speaking so openly about my self-hate, and an unexpected gratitude that Cian would care enough to make sure I was all right after reading that shit. I'd been incredibly unfair with all the assumptions I'd made about him, pretty much since day one. He was kind, caring, and one of the most genuine people I'd ever met.

"So about this friend thing," I said.

He blinked, visibly changing gears in his mind.

"What about it?"

"Well, what would it involve?"

His mouth twitched, eyes sparkling as he slid his hands a little higher on my thighs.

"Surprise outings, meals together, unexpected drop-ins... you know. The usual friend things."

It was my turn to blink.

"You already do all of that."

I hadn't once invited him to spend time with me. He just turned up and dragged me into whatever he'd decided we were doing. Secretly, I loved it.

"That's because we're already friends. I was just waiting for you to catch up."

The laugh that burst out of me was warm and light, clearing pockets of darkness in me that had curdled over the years.

"Okay," I said, biting my lip to give me courage, "but can we talk about a benefit package?"

The groan that rumbled out of his chest was half feral as he palmed my ass and dragged me forward until I was perched over a very large bulge in his jeans.

"Fuck, yes. Please."

This time, I took control, wrapping my hands around his face and lowering my smiling lips to his. He tasted like soy sauce as I licked into his mouth, teasing him with my tongue. His fingers curled against my ass, and in response, I rocked my hips over his erection.

Fuck the haters.

Fuck my family.

Fuck my self-loathing.

I wanted Cian O'Leary, and while he wanted me, he could damn well have me.

His hands wandered up my back, growing bolder with each pass until they slid beneath my shirt and palmed my breasts. I broke away from him with a curse, whipping off my shirt and tugging at the hem of his, eager to do some exploring of my own.

FIFTEEN

Cian

HER SMALL HANDS traced lines over my chest and abs, the touch so light it raised goosebumps on my heated flesh. Fuck, yes. I'd wanted this for a while now. Dreamed about moments like this. But reality was so much better.

Her tits were a perfect handful beneath her practical cotton bra, and my mouth watered at the prospect of being able to taste her. They'd been so close when she was determined to get her phone that I deserved a gold medal for resisting the urge to bite them. Suck them into my mouth and learn all the noises she could make.

She swiveled her hips, and I dropped my head back with a soft moan.

"Do that again." My voice was low and full of gravel, but she complied so sweetly, moving over me with more confidence. Her lips parted on a soft pant, and I gave in to temptation, pressing a chaste kiss to her lips before working along her jaw and dipping to suck on the skin of her collarbone.

"Yes." She fisted a hand in my hair, guiding me to where she wanted my mouth.

I bit at her pebbled nipple through the thin fabric of her bra, laving my tongue over the cotton until it was see-through. It wasn't enough. Keeping one hand on her hip to encourage her movements, I used the other to unhook and discard the unwanted barrier between us.

Her whimper as I sucked her flesh into my mouth was everything.

"Ride me, baby. Take what you need," I growled, moving my attention to her other breast as she let out a keening sound and worked her pussy harder against my dick.

Why were we wearing pants?

I lapped at her, alternating between sharp nips and soothing licks until she threw her head back with a shout.

Her face glowed as she shuddered above me, and I willed myself to calm the fuck down. We weren't going to come in our jeans. This wasn't even about me. It was about earning her trust. About earning more with her.

She dropped her forehead to my shoulder, breathing hard as small aftershocks shook her body.

Wrapping my arms around her, I held her close, breathing in her lavender scent and marveling at how lucky I was to have her attention. As her breathing calmed and she kept right where she was, I tried to catch a look at her face. Beneath her mess of curls, her ears were red.

"Well," she said into my shoulder, refusing to give me her eyes. "That just happened."

"It sure did."

She huffed, and the warm breath tickled over my throat.

"Can we pretend it didn't?" The hope in her voice was cute, but there wasn't a chance I was letting her pull away from me now. Emotionally, anyway.

She shifted off my lap, and I mostly kept the wince to myself. A light breeze was going to feel erotic as hell until I had the chance to rub out this boner.

"Oh, shit. You didn't... of course you didn't." Her eyes shuttered as she shifted back against the arm of the sofa.

"Hey." I reached for her hand, trying to draw her back in.

"Just because I'm not keen on making a mess of the only clothing I have here doesn't mean I didn't love the hell out of that. You're so fucking sexy when you come, and honestly, I deserve some kind of prize because I'm so close to the edge here."

Her eyes dropped to my dick, who decided to try reaching for her himself when I stayed put. Yup, my body had no doubt about who we wanted.

"I could take care of it, if you want."

Fuck, yes, we want!

"This isn't about me."

Wrong thing to say. She folded her arms around her bare breasts, hiding them from my view.

"Shit. Blair. I'm not saying this right. I'm so fucking in for friends with benefits, but I don't want you thinking I *only* want to fuck you."

Her eyes were wary behind those pretty gold-framed glasses and she relaxed the tiniest bit.

"But you do want to fuck me?"

"It isn't obvious?" I waved my hand at my dick, as it tried to wave at her.

She slid to the floor and maneuvered her body between my knees.

Seriously, a man was only so strong.

Silently giving myself over to her, I stretched my arms along the back of the sofa as she worked my button and zipper with efficient hands. I lifted my hips to help as she slid down my jeans and boxers, and my erection sprang free. The relief from the pressure of my clothing was nothing compared to the warm, wet slide of her mouth over my head.

Fuuuuuuck.

Do not embarrass yourself.

I clenched my ass hard and tried to think of my junior hockey stats to bring me back from the edge as she wrapped her fist around the base of my cock and tongued my slit before sucking me all the way back into her throat.

I didn't want to think about how she'd gotten so good at this. Some ungrateful bastard had used her without appreciating the absolute queen she was. Because if they had, they never would have let her go.

I wasn't stupid. We'd call this whatever she wanted us to: friends with benefits, boyfriend/girlfriend, whatever. But one thing was crystal clear for me.

I was hers.

And if she wanted to leave me, I'd put up a hell of a fight to keep her.

"Your mouth feels amazing."

She did something with her tongue and I tried to remember the alphabet backward in a panicked rush so it wouldn't be over.

Please don't let it be over.

Her grasp was firm, her fist sliding easily over my length with the amount of spit slicking me up.

Fuck, forget first loves and passionate one-night stands; this was the single greatest sexual encounter of my life.

And her pants were still on.

I wondered if she'd let me go down on her. I bet she'd taste like heaven.

Shit.

The image that came with that thought fanned the burning in my lower back into an inferno.

"I'm coming," I choked out, trying to give her warning before I lost it. She tightened her fist and kept sucking as I lost the battle and my orgasm rolled over me like a freight train.

The sight of her lips stretched wide, her throat working to swallow what I gave her drew it out until I felt empty in the best kind of way.

"Holy shit," I breathed, wondering if she would be offended if I just laid down on the sofa and passed out for a while.

She pulled off me slowly, releasing my spent cock with a gentle pop, then sat back on her heels and licked her lips.

My body shuddered, and my dick made a valiant effort to rally at the sight, but while the spirit was willing, the flesh was weak... at least for the next twenty minutes.

"Come here, my queen." I folded myself onto the sofa and tucked her against me so she was the little spoon to my big. For a few long minutes, we lay together and breathed. Peace stole over me as I felt her heartbeat slow beneath my palm and my eyelids drooped.

"I really like this friends with benefits thing," she whispered.

I hummed. We'd DTR later, but for now, as long as she was happy, so was I.

My last thought before we both fell asleep was that I'd have to encourage Blair to start bonding with Seelie.

Both my beautiful, misunderstood girls deserved the best.

I woke sometime later to a much darker room. Blair was still snoozing in my arms, and my pants were still around my knees. Classy, O'Leary.

We'd left the sushi out while we were sidetracked by more enjoyable things, and as much as I wanted to stay right where I was, the thought of room temperature fish was enough to make me slide out from behind Blair and clean up the mess we'd made.

After I fixed my pants.

I started with the lunch mess, then moved into the kitchen, washing the few dishes in the sink, then checked the apartment for more cups. Blair was a drink goblin, and wasn't that adorable. After the dishes were all clean and put away, I started to fold the clothing draped over her dining table.

"What are you doing?" Her voice was rough with sleep, her hair wild, and there were small indents on her face where her glasses had pressed into her skin.

"You're beautiful."

She rolled her eyes.

"You don't have to sweet talk me. I already sucked your cock."

Why did she always try to cheapen...

"Sorry," she said, reading my displeasure.

"Please try to believe what I tell you. I promise, if I want to fuck you, I'll just say it. I won't try to win you over with pretty words. I'm a simple guy, and I don't like games."

She looked down at the pile of folded laundry I'd made,

then glanced at the coffee table that was free of food, then at the clean kitchen.

"I'm trying. It's just not something I'm used to. I don't take compliments well, and I have a habit of negatively translating them in my head. I told Dante today that I'm going to find a therapist."

"I think that's a great idea."

She laughed. "Everyone says that. Am I that fucked up?"

She was deflecting again. I shook my head.

"No, but everyone needs someone to talk to. Whether they're a professional, or a friend. Our support networks keep us level and tell us what we need to hear. In a related matter, I do, in fact, want to fuck you. Just thought you should know."

Her laugh was exactly what I'd been aiming for, and as she moved in and wrapped her arms around me, I felt ten feet tall.

"Are you hungry?" I asked, thinking of the sushi we'd wasted. Maybe we could go for tacos.

Her eyes heated, her hands sliding to my ass as she cocked her head at me.

"For food." I laughed.

"Hmmm, I ate plenty before, but I guess we could go somewhere." Shit. The innuendo in her voice went straight to my cock and I wondered if I could still get blue balls after coming so hard a couple of hours before. How the hell had this vixen hidden in plain sight for so long?

"Let me feed you, then we can see where the night takes us."

"Deal."

She pulled away, and I immediately missed her closeness. What the hell had she done to me?

It was like some bonding by osmosis thing. Maybe it happened while we slept.

Or maybe it had been there all along, and that was why Oscar constantly accused me of stalking.

While she ducked into her bedroom to freshen up, I used her bathroom and planned out our dinner date. We had an early flight the next day, so as much as I wanted to learn her body more, it would have to wait until after Finland. But we had five days off when we got home, and I was going to make the most of them.

CHAPTER
SIXTEEN

Blair

THE GLOBAL SERIES had been a bust. Florida kicked our boys all over the ice, and it was a somber flight home for everyone. We landed at the Austin-Bergstrom International Airport jetlagged and dejected. Coach Mack debriefed the guys on the tarmac before wishing them a restful week off, reminding them to get their training in and "for fuck's sake, make sure you fly under the radar."

He'd been pissed about the photo of Cian and me, but it had been for similar reasons to Cian and Dante. The public was a necessary evil, but they were assholes who shouldn't have a say in how the players spent their spare time. Especially because eating at a diner wasn't the scandal it had been made out to be.

"Can I come over tonight?" Cian muttered in my ear as we waited for our bags to be unloaded.

"Aren't you exhausted?"

His grin was devious, and I rolled my eyes, feigning annoyance.

"You're just going to turn up anyway, aren't you?"

He chuckled. "This way you get a lift home."

I grinned at him, quickly hiding the expression when I noticed Dante watching us.

Shit.

It looked like I should give her an update, if I wanted to keep my promise.

"I'll meet you outside," I said, giving his hand a subtle squeeze before I moved through the crush of players to get to my mentor.

"Status change?" she asked without preamble as I reached her side.

"Friends," I said firmly, glancing around to see who was in earshot.

"With benefits?"

I'd promised her honesty, but still felt a little like a schoolgirl talking to her principal as I gave a sharp nod.

"Hey." She grasped my elbow, ducking her head so she could meet my eyes. "As long as you're both happy, that's all we care about. We'll plan for the worst, but make sure you enjoy the ride. Okay?"

I let my shoulders drop, giving her a thankful smile.

"Yeah. Yeah, I will. I just... yeah." I ran out of words, unable to express how much I wanted this thing to work for as long as it could. Dante's unwavering support made me feel less like an idiot for even trying.

"Hey, Disney princess," Chet called.

"Fuck off, Doyle," Cian replied, yanking his bag off the trolley.

"I mean, you got the hair for it, Beauty."

"Give it a rest, Doyle," Mack warned.

Dante sighed, murmuring about asshole players under her breath as she retrieved her own bag.

"Just wanted to wish him well, maybe warn him against trespassing in any beast's castles." He sniggered, swinging his gaze to me, as if anyone could misinterpret the implication.

"How the fuck do you know so much about cartoons, Doyle? You rubbing one out to the tune of *Be Our Guest* or some shit?" Oscar asked, eliciting laughter and jeers from the rest of the team.

He winked at me as we made eye contact, and once again I was reminded why the giant winger was one of my favorite people. His wife was awesome, too.

Dante and I left the banter behind as we headed for the parking lot.

"Enjoy your time off and ignore all the stupid coming from the peanut gallery, okay?"

I gave her a quick hug and headed toward Cian's truck, Dante's advice ringing in my head.

I knew what I was getting into. The good, the bad, and the ugly. And I wasn't talking about myself because I'd promised Cian I'd make a conscious effort to challenge my negative thoughts. I'd also Googled therapists in my area while we were away and booked a time to meet with one later in the week to see if we were a good fit. It was about time I started claiming my life instead of whining about my past and things I couldn't change.

I threw my bags into the truck bed and climbed into the passenger seat, letting out an embarrassing squeak when Cian immediately pulled me into a hard kiss.

"I've wanted to do that for two days," he murmured against my lips.

"Then you'd better get us home."

He released me immediately and cranked his engine while I strapped on my seat belt.

The drive took longer than I wanted it to. Every traffic light in between the airport and my apartment seemed to be in on some kind of plan to teach us delayed gratification, to the point where I considered ordering Cian to pull into an empty parking lot so I could get some relief.

The only thing that stopped me was the fact I wanted him inside me, and Cian was the kind of guy that would nix any plan to have our first time in the back of his truck.

Finally. *Finally*, we pulled into the parking lot of my apartment, and the truck was barely in park before I opened my door and slid to the ground.

"Let me just... Nope, she's gone." Cian's chuckle followed me to the front door where I waved him into the building impatiently, squirming in my wet panties. He lugged both of our overnight bags up the three flights, and the second we stepped into my apartment, I threw myself at him. He was right there to catch me, lifting me onto his hips as his tongue drove into my mouth.

Without further direction, he carried me down the hall and into my bedroom, crawling up the bed until my head hit the pillows beneath his hard body.

"Should we shower?" I asked. We weren't exactly fresh after a ten-hour flight.

"Don't care. I need you." He kissed me, then slipped my jeans and panties off, following the fabric down until he settled between my legs.

"Fuck, you're soaked for me," he murmured, dragging a finger over my opening and holding it up.

"Will you let me eat this sweet pussy, Blair?"

None of the men I'd had sex with in the past had wanted to go down on me. The nicer ones made me come with their fingers, but this was something else. It felt more intimate, somehow.

Cian sucked his wet finger into his mouth, letting out a pleasured hum as he licked over the digit like it was a candy apple.

"Please."

Why did that word always make me want to give him anything he asked?

"Okay."

With a growl, he buried his face in my folds, sending sparks of heat through my whole body as he licked and sucked my clit the same way he had my breasts last time we were together.

"Oh, shit," I whimpered, overwhelmed with sensation. The scrape of his beard on my sensitive flesh, his tongue spearing into my opening then laving over my clit. He shifted his weight, pushing two fingers into my pussy as he lapped at me in hard strokes. Without conscious thought, my hips lifted to meet his mouth, a silent plea for more.

He hummed, and the vibrations ratcheted up the heat pooling in my belly. "You taste fucking amazing. I knew you would. Fuck, I'm going to need more of this."

He crooked his fingers, sucking on my clit as I came so hard my voice broke on a scream. My heart thundered in my chest. Chills of pleasure sparked through my body as he gentled the strokes of his tongue, fingers moving lazily in and out of me, prolonging the sensations until I was so sensitive I had to push his hand away.

I cursed, my body continuing to shudder as he lifted himself back over me and took my lips in a sinful kiss. I could taste my release on his tongue, a primitive part of me loving the fact I'd marked him in some small way.

"Ohh, shit. I need you."

I locked my ankles around his hips, rubbing my wet pussy against his dress pants. The fine woolen texture made me pant, but it wasn't enough.

"Then take me," I ground out, tugging at his clothing, wanting nothing more than to have him naked above me. In me. Taking us both up to that edge that was sweet pain and completion.

He kneeled up, pulling his wallet from his back pocket and retrieving a condom.

"Thank God," he muttered, like he wasn't sure he'd had one.

He stripped out of his shirt, pants, and boxers, and rolled the rubber over his thick head while I took in his immaculate body. The training regime players were subjected to, combined with the hours of game time during the season, had crafted his body into over six feet of pure muscle. His chest and abs looked like something carved by classical artists, while his ass was so round and firm I barely resisted the urge to bite it. The thought that I didn't deserve his attention tried to surface, but I gave it a vicious shove as he settled between my thighs and positioned himself at my opening.

"Are you ready?" he asked, keeping eye contact and pushing in on a slow thrust at my nod. He was big. The jaw ache I'd had the day after our first hookup was testament to that, but I was so wet, so ready for him, that he slid in easily and we both breathed a sigh as his hips nestled in against mine.

"I'm going to live here," he murmured, pumping his hips in tiny pulses so he stayed seated deep inside me.

"Do you mean in my apartment? Or my pussy?"

"I wouldn't invite myself to live in your apartment, but it may happen as a consequence of wanting to stay inside you forever. Might be a difficult sell to the team for the rest of the season, but I'm sure we'll manage."

I laughed at the boyish grin he shot me, the noise transforming into a moan as he pulled almost all the way out and pushed back in slowly.

I never thought Cian would be a playful lover. Powerful, considerate, dominating, yes, but playful?

"Fuck, you take me so well," he gritted out, grasping the headboard for leverage as he picked up his pace. I whined in reply, reaching between us to rub the building ache from my clit.

"Oh, shit, yes. Rub your clit. I want you to make yourself come on my dick."

He shifted to his knees and palmed my ass to drive in deeper while giving me room to get myself to the edge.

"I can feel you clamping down on me so tight. Come for me, Blair. Make my cock wet with your juices so I can lick them up and we can start again."

My eyes rolled back in my head as his words took me over the edge, and I felt, as much as heard his groan when he gathered me into his chest and held me through my shuddering release. When my body settled, he pulled out and scooted down the bed.

"Oh, God. Cian." I whimpered as his tongue smoothed over my lips, dipping inside before moving up to tease my clit.

"Hmmm, I've been dreaming of this. Can you give me one more? I want to finish inside you, but I want you to come on my tongue again first."

"Damn. Athletic. Endurance," I panted, rocking my hips against his mouth as he nipped at me. I felt his grin against my pussy as he took me past the point of no return again.

When I was nothing more than a puddle of over-pleasured Blair, he pushed back into my swollen pussy once more and finally let himself come with a shuddering moan.

He rolled to the side, pulling me in toward his body so that my head rested against his pec. His heart thundered beneath my cheek and I couldn't suppress the grin that spread across my face. I'd fought my demons tonight, and had the best sex of my life as a reward.

It didn't matter what came next because Cian had awoken something in me that I thought my family had killed a long time ago.

I was ready to take control of my life.

And fuck the haters.

SEVENTEEN

Cian

I woke up the next morning with aching muscles and a hard dick. Beneath me, a warm body wriggled against my not so little problem, giving the dumb handle the idea that it might be time for round two.

But if I was sore, Blair must be ready to bring out the bath salts and heat rub. I hadn't gone easy on her last night. In fact, I'd been an absolute caveman. There was just something about her that had me addicted. With a herculean effort, I pulled my hips back so she could rest without being poked in the ass, but she followed, grinding against me in a way that had me tightening my grip on her. Was she awake?

I couldn't tell, and as much as I wanted to roll her over and take her, I didn't think we were at that level of familiarity yet.

Maybe we could have the conversation today, and in the future, I could wake her up with my tongue. My erection kicked against her ass, keen to make the idea a reality sooner rather than later.

I smoothed her hair back from her face, noting how much younger she looked without her glasses on. How reliant was she on them? I'd never asked, but I'd also never seen her without them.

She blinked her eyes open, squinting up at me with a cute little crease between her brows.

"I'm hungry," I whispered, running my hand down her belly to cup her pussy in case she needed help with what I wanted to eat.

"You're insatiable. And I need a shower before we do any more... eating."

I grinned, taking it as a maybe, and pushed out of bed to start the shower.

There was a scraping sound and a groan, and as I glanced over my shoulder, she blinked through her glasses at me, gaze fixed firmly on my ass.

We cleaned up quickly, then I dropped to my knees and dirtied her up a couple of times before she returned the favor. By the time we toweled off, we were both flushed despite the water having gone cold several minutes before we finished.

"We should start going to my place," I said, scrubbing the towel through my hair. "Unlimited hot water, and no neighbors to get into our business."

I dried off my legs and straightened to find her staring at me.

"I don't even know where you live."

She didn't know...? We had started, or ended, here every time we'd hung out, so of course she didn't know.

"I'm in Barton Creek, around the corner from Oscar and Mia. We should go there tonight."

She nodded slowly, her face screwed up the way it did when she was overthinking something. Did she think I'd been trying to hide her? Surely not, I'd literally sent my friends in to advocate for us. Still...

"I've been coming to you because you're central. I want you in my space, though. Maybe we can have a cookout, or invite some friends over for dinner."

"That sounds kind of couple-y, doesn't it?"

It did, but that's because I was warming her up to the idea of being a couple. Slow and steady. Don't spook her.

"Friends have dinner together all the time."

She didn't believe me, but she didn't have to, as long as she agreed.

Dropping her towel, she slipped into her panties and another soft cotton bra and wandered out of the bathroom. I picked up after her, hanging both her towel and mine side by side on the rack, then followed her into the bedroom.

"What's on your agenda today?" The question was muffled as she pulled a sweater over her head, her wet curls making an appearance before her face popped through the collar.

"Ahh, I'm supposed to meet Oscar at the training center at ten to get our workout in, then I'm going to spend some time with Seelie. I'll see if Oscar and Mia want to come around tonight for dinner, then I'll sit by the phone like a lost puppy waiting to see if you join us."

She laughed, like I hoped she would and bent to pull a pair of pants out of her drawer.

I bit my knuckle, but a moan still slipped out at the sight of her sweet ass, and the thin panel of fabric covering that pussy I could still taste on my tongue.

"Change of plans. Get on the bed."

She laughed, ignoring the erection that had popped up between us and finished getting dressed.

"Are clothes in your plans today? Because I don't think my neighbors will warm to you if you go around looking like that." She paused, chewing her lip.

"Or maybe they will. I'd better take care of that for you. You can say thanks by giving me a ride into work and shouting coffee."

She wrapped her hand around my hard dick, pushing up onto her toes to lick at my lips before she sank to her knees and swallowed me whole. One hand pumped me into her mouth while the other tugged and rolled at my balls.

Don't thrust. Don't thrust.

I widened my stance and balled my hands by my sides, praying for restraint as she scraped her teeth along my shaft.

She released me with a pop, looking up at me with pre-cum glistening on her lip.

"I won't break. Use me."

Reaching out to take my hand, she guided it to her hair and resumed blowing my mind. I thrust cautiously, trying to test the limits of her gag reflex, but then she grunted and dug her blunt fingernails into my ass and I let go.

Hinging at the hips, I drove into her mouth, loving the sloppy wet sounds she made. Her hand crept down the front of her pants and I groaned as she thrust against her palm in time to my strokes in her mouth.

"Coming," I grunted, looking around for a towel, in case she didn't want... those fingernails bit deeper and I lost my rhythm as I came in pulsing waves that threatened to buckle my knees.

"Where have you been all my life," I rasped as I hauled her to her feet. Her tongue tasted of bitter salt, and knowing that a part of me would be inside her today made me feral.

"Tell me you'll come tonight," I demanded as I shoved my hand down her pants and finished her off. She gave me a lazy grin.

Watching for her response, I reluctantly pulled away and dug fresh clothing out of my overnight bag.

"Tell me where to go, and I'll be there."

"Good answer. Now, get your butt in the car so we can get this day done."

OSCAR AGREED to dinner as we sweated our way through a cardio session, and grilled me on the state of things with Blair.

"Come tonight and see for yourself." Was all I said, and I knew he was going to find a way to retaliate at some point in the near future.

I was prepared for it.

I spent a few hours at the shelter with Seelie, surprised to be greeted with a small tail wag when I sat in her cage. After only a few minutes, she army crawled out of her nest and curled up against my leg, barely flinching when I stroked her flank.

I told her about Blair. About how much I liked her and wanted her to be mine.

Seelie let out a soft snore and a fart that rivaled anything that could come out of a locker room.

"Shit, Seelie. What are they feeding you?"

I waved a hand over my nose, praying for the smell to dissipate as my eyes watered.

"How are we doing in here?" Katie asked, recoiling as the smell hit her.

"She's good. Stinky, but good. Is it time to lock up?"

The shelter closed to the public at four PM daily to give staff a chance to have vets in and clean the enclosures of the less friendly animals without risking people who hadn't signed indemnity waivers.

I shuffled away from the sleeping canine, my heart hurting when she startled awake and bolted to her nest of bedding.

"She trusts you so much."

"Yeah. I'm terrified of fuc—er, I mean screwing it up."

"I'm old enough to hear you swear, Grandpa," she sassed, lightly punching my shoulder.

"I'm only eight years older than you, you know."

"Yeah, like I said."

"Kids these days." I shook my head in mock disappointment and headed for the exit.

Traffic was light, and I made good time getting home, stopping at our local grocery store for supplies on the way. I'd already texted Blair my address and told her to come when she could, and the bar fridge was full of a variety of beer and soda.

I double checked the ice trays and looked around my little home. What would Blair think of it?

Admittedly, I hadn't personalized it a whole lot since moving in. While Oscar and Mia's house was full of knickknacks and memorabilia from trips they'd taken and homey furnishings Mia had used to brighten up the place, mine still had the paintings that came with the house and the original wall colors.

Did it look too much like a museum? I'd never cared to show off my trophies and medals from my years in hockey, and despite living alone, I always felt as though I'd be taking up space having them out collecting dust.

The front door creaked open, and Oscar and Mia strode in, arms laden with food.

"I told you not to bring anything," I said, pecking a kiss on Mia's cheek and slapping Oscar's back.

"I was working out a routine in my head today, so I baked. And roasted."

The slow roasted beef smelled amazing, and a glimpse under the cover on the second tray revealed cinnamon buns.

"Since when can you cook?" I asked, remembering the early days when Oscar had been in charge of their diet.

"You're looking at my entire repertoire. Enjoy."

I chuckled, retrieving two beers and a soda from the fridge.

"So... Is she here?" Mia asked, close on my heels.

"Not yet, but hopefully soon?" A knock at the door interrupted me. Mia let out a squeal and rushed to let in the last guest.

"Don't scare her off."

She returned a couple of minutes later with a wide-eyed Blair in tow.

"This place is really nice."

"I'll show you around." Mia took her by the elbow, leading her through my too-small-to-need-a-tour home. I headed out to the back deck where Oscar had already pulled up a chair in the outdoor dining area.

"You don't need to hover. Mia's been desperate for you to find someone, and she likes Blair. She won't do anything to screw you over."

Was I that obvious?

"It's all so new, I feel like I'm walking in a minefield. It's bad enough she wants to label us friends with benefits. How long before I can tell her we're dating?"

Oscar snorted.

"Maybe wait for her to bring up that conversation. She seems almost as skittish as Mia was."

I grunted, sipping at my beer.

I could be patient.

Maybe.

But I couldn't handle the idea that something outside of my control might blow this whole thing up in my face. It had been a near miss with that social post, but what if people got louder? Bolder? What if they said that shit to Blair's face and she believed it that way she believed the shit her family told her? I was going to drive myself crazy with all this questioning, so for tonight, I would enjoy good friends and good food. Tomorrow, I could work out how to make the ground beneath us more solid.

Blair's laugh drifted from inside, and I wondered what they were talking about.

"I'm making myself crazy," I growled, dropping my head in my hands.

"Welcome to love, my man." Oscar raised his beer in a toast and took a long pull.

"Love? No, I'm not..." I thought about how I felt toward Blair. The urge to possess her. Needing to be near her and talk to her and hear what she'd done while she was away from me.

"No," I said definitively, because who the hell fell in love this quickly.

"Whatever, man. I'm just calling it as I see it."

"Fuck off."

"Maybe you need to touch some grass."

I flipped him off as the girls joined us. Apparently,

they'd found the fixings I'd bought for a charcuterie board. Mia held the cheese board that had been on display when I bought the house, and along its length, cheese, sausage, olives and crackers sat in neat little rows. Blair had two sodas in her hands, and passed one to Mia as they settled across from us.

"This house is gorgeous," she said, knocking her foot against mine as she shifted in her chair. "It's small, but with how often we're away, it's enough."

"Hmm."

Oscar started up a conversation at that point about some flamenco dance night he and Mia were heading to, and I sat back to watch as Blair interacted with my friends. She was funny and thoughtful as she asked questions designed to keep the conversation flowing. Some of the things she asked I didn't even know the answer to, and I'd known them for forever.

As the sun set, I excused myself and prepared dinner, returning with platters of meat and vegetables that we all picked at as conversation moved to the rest of the season and upcoming events.

"Are you going to the Thanksgiving event?" Blair asked.

"The charity? Yeah, I'm... really keen to help orphans." Mia smiled sadly as Oscar rubbed her back. I didn't know much about her childhood, but it hadn't been great. Maybe she understood what those kids were going through better than any of us.

"How about you?"

Blair grinned. "I'll be there with bells on. Especially because it means I won't be around for my own family's Thanksgiving dinner."

The girls shared a knowing look and changed the subject to lighter things.

The sun was long set, the table cleared and dishes washed and put away when Oscar and Mia made their excuses and headed for the door.

"I had a really great night. It was lovely getting to know you better, Blair," Mia said as they hugged a brief farewell.

"Me too," Blair replied with a shy smile.

I waved goodbye to my friends, closing the door once they reached their car, then turned to my girl.

"So I know Mia gave you the tour, but did you see the bedroom?"

She pursed her lips, fighting a smile as I stepped into her space.

"Y'know, I'm not so sure. Do you think you could remind me?" she asked, backing out of arm's reach.

"Run."

She let out a small shriek, curls bouncing as she sprinted toward the back of my house.

I caught her at the door to the bedroom and threw her on the bed.

And introduced her to my bedroom a half dozen times.

EIGHTEEN

Blair

"ARE YOU COMING TO O'MALLEY'S?" Cian was practically vibrating out of his skin, his adrenaline high after their win against Boston, and I laughed as he backed me into a corner outside the locker room.

"Someone might see us."

We'd spent almost every night together in the last two weeks, and with the amount of energy he was exuding, I knew we'd be burning off some steam sooner rather than later. Going to the bar seemed like an exercise in delayed gratification, but I couldn't deny the idea of being out in public with Cian was exhilarating.

"Who cares? It's no one's business but ours. Come out with me. Please?" He widened his eyes, giving me a hangdog expression that was so freaking cute, he knew I couldn't tell him no. When I held out, he dropped his head to my neck and nipped at my skin, making my nipples harden and my panties wet.

Bastard.

"Yes, we'll go. Pack up your things and I'll meet you at your truck."

It had become habit to let him drive me around, to the point where my car hadn't needed gas in weeks. I'd offered to chip in, but he pretended not to hear me.

I pushed him away with a soft smile and headed back to where I'd left my bag and equipment, raw footage ready to be formatted and spread to the masses for likes and shares.

As I shouldered my pack, my phone vibrated in my pocket. Expecting it to be Cian in all his eternal impatience, I answered with a smile.

"Hey."

"My daughter lives. Thanks be to God. Where the hell have you been, Duckie? Too important to call your mother back so we don't think you're dead in a ditch somewhere? I guess you aren't as smart as we thought. Either that, or you don't care about the people who raised you."

Goddamn it. My mood plummeted as my mother's favorite rant about how I was the worst daughter in existence continued.

"Look, Mom, you know how busy I get once the season starts," I cut in.

"Your sister is on set and she still finds time to call. You know she's dating a football player now. We're all gathering for Thanksgiving. Make sure you're there."

I'd never been so glad to have to wear heels for something.

"I have a charity event on Thanksgiving."

"That's fine. Georgia can't make it until the thirtieth. I already checked, and you don't have a game that night so you can get your ungrateful butt home and see your family."

I didn't want to go.

Things were always worse when I saw them in person. Especially if Georgia had found someone to bring home to Mom and Dad. I needed backup. I needed someone who would...

The solution hit me so hard I gasped, looking around in case anyone knew what I was thinking. Friends with benefits wasn't an arrangement that needed to be common knowledge in the club.

"I'm bringing a plus-one."

Silence greeted my declaration. Like what I'd said was so absurd she had to check the connection.

"Mom?"

It was my turn to check my phone, but apparently, I hadn't shocked my mother into silence for too long.

"Sure. Bring whoever you want, but I expect you to be here at five PM sharp. You know your father likes to eat early."

"How is Dad?" I asked. The only person under that roof I cared about took his role as patriarch seriously. He was the breadwinner. He worked all day, expected dinner on the table when he got home, and had always treated me as the son he never had. We bonded over a shared love of hockey, and while he would never interfere in the way Mom chose to raise us, my childhood had included brief moments of reprieve from the incessant judgment of my mother in the form of bonding time with dad.

"Still breathing. I would have done less time for murder." She huffed at her own shitty joke and wrapped up the call with another warning to remember the date.

All in all, it was one of the better phone calls I'd had with her.

I wandered outside, wondering how to ask Cian to play

backup with my family when even I didn't want to go.

"You ready?" he asked as I climbed into the cab.

"Yup."

"What's wrong?"

A flippant comment was on the tip of my tongue, ready to deflect from my shitty life when I remembered I'd promised him the truth.

"I accidentally answered a call from my mom."

He hissed through his teeth in sympathy.

"My attendance is expected at the family Thanksgiving dinner."

"But we have—"

"I know." I held up a hand to stop him.

"They're planning it around Georgia's schedule, so it's happening on the thirtieth. She already made sure I didn't have an out."

He nodded slowly as he pulled out from the curb and steered us toward the Irish Pub that was his team's second home.

"Okay, so we go, eat some food, then make an excuse to leave as soon as humanly possible."

"We?"

He looked at me like I had a screw loose.

"You want to do this by yourself? I'm not okay with that."

I rubbed my hands together in my lap and, once again, wondered what the hell I'd done to deserve him.

"No, I was going to ask you to come. But I thought I'd have to warm you up to the idea."

He turned his blinker on and steered around the corner one handed as he reached across the cab and grasped my wrist.

"Friends don't let other friends go into toxic situations alone."

He squeezed me firmly before returning his hands to the wheel while he searched for a parking space.

"Thank you."

O'Malley's was as loud and crowded as always, people jostling for position at the bar while others milled and chatted in the middle of high traffic areas. Cian pulled me in front of him, wrapping an arm firmly around my waist as he used the other to herd the crowd out of the way. It was a tactic I never could have employed, but seeing as he was here to do it for me, I didn't mind as much as I normally would.

"O'Leary!" Shouts of his name turned heads around the room as he found us a couple of chairs and poured me a drink from the nearest pitcher before serving himself.

We relaxed together, rehashing the game with his teammates as they crowed with delight over the highlights. I was on my second beer when it happened. Cian was animatedly describing a successful deke Miller had pulled off when a mini skirt-clad ass pushed in between us. The voluptuous brunette bent close to Cian's ear, whispering God knew what, but the motion forced me back to avoid her ass in my face. The bunny invited herself into his lap, snapping away with her phone as her hand wandered over his chest.

The same chest I'd scratched up the night before when I'd ridden for an hour after he'd interrupted my work.

Jealousy flared white hot, and I tried to remind myself I had no claim over him just because we were friends with benefits. He could have the same arrangement with others if he wanted to. Chest tight, I pushed my chair away, ready to make a break for it when a familiar hand circled my wrist.

"That's enough," Cian said to the girl whose hand was drifting lower and lower.

"But..."

He helped her to her feet one handed and tugged me into the space she had just been.

"Cian," I chided as he pulled me into his lap, ignoring the disgruntled noise the bunny made behind him.

"Duckie."

"Don't call me that."

"Why? It's cute, like you."

He buried his face in my hair, mouth seeking my neck as I wondered how many drinks he'd had.

"Can we go home now? I want to fall asleep with my dick inside you."

"Cian."

"Will you let me in bare? I want to see your hole dripping with my cum. I'll fuck you awake in the morning and send you to work with panties dripping in my seed." He groaned, rolling his hips underneath me, letting me feel how hard he was.

Laughter interrupted the growing lust between us. Wyatt Whitney, our fourth line winger, grabbed a curvy girl with a blonde ponytail who looked familiar—maybe from the stadium?—and kissed her soundly. She whispered something to him, and I barely heard him reply, "That's all I want. You and me. Happy." They grinned at each other like there was no one else in the room, and the way they both jumped when someone cleared their throat confirmed the suspicion. Love surrounded the pair like a cloak of protection and my eyes felt misty as Cian's hand rubbed over my stomach. Would I ever find something like that?

His fingers danced along the inseam of my jeans, and I decided there was enough time for what-ifs later. For now, I had to get my own *it's complicated* relationship safely home.

"Come on, big man. Time to go."

He was only too happy to comply, pasting himself, and his erection, to my back as we negotiated the crowd and made it outside to his truck.

"Keys, please."

The fact he handed them over was a surprise.

"Thanks, Duckie. You're so good to me." He settled in his seat as I adjusted everything on my side so I could reach the pedals.

"Damn long legs," I bitched as I slid all the way forward.

The drive home was the longest of my life, everything seeming tiny before the giant wheels of the truck. I felt like the king of the road. I chose to take us to my apartment for convenience—a much shorter drive and less likelihood I'd mess up his truck—but Cian had already fallen asleep by the time we pulled in. Between the adrenaline crash after the game and the beers he'd drank, it wasn't a surprise, but I wouldn't let him sleep here and potentially wake up sore.

"We're home." I shook him gently. When he didn't move, because he was one hundred and eighty pounds of pure muscle, I shook harder.

"Love you, Duckie," he murmured, shifting around until his head rested against the window.

I froze, hand raised to shake him again as I ran through a series of reinterpretations.

Because there is no way that drunk, sleepy Cian O'Leary had just said he loved me.

Maybe he had a plush animal he'd loved as a kid.

The excuse barely held water, but it was enough for me to shake off the shock and punch his shoulder.

"Wake up."

"Hey," he rumbled, scrubbing a hand down his face. "Oh, we're home. Did I fall asleep?"

Instead of answering, I jumped out of the truck, belatedly remembering I should have moved the seat back for him. Oh well, he'd deal with it later.

My skin felt itchy as I stalked across the parking lot, and an irrational titration settled in as I waited for him to join me. I hit the central locking system to ensure his truck would still be there in the morning and climbed the stairs behind him to my apartment.

Once inside, I made myself busy in the kitchen, pouring him water and retrieving a bottle of Tylenol from the back of the cupboard.

"I didn't have that much to drink," he protested, though he drank all the water down in a gulp and helped himself to a second glass from the tap.

"I didn't say you did."

"What's wrong?" He cornered me against the counter, forcing eye contact as his bulky arms caged me in.

"Nothing. I'm just tired. Long day."

He tilted his head, studying me in a way that made me think he hadn't been as drunk as I thought. The implications of that were too much for me to handle at that moment, so I tilted my chin up and dared him to challenge me.

"Do you want me to go home?"

"No."

He nodded, as if wanting his presence was enough for now. Maybe it was. Exhaustion stole over me, giving truth to my excuse as I dragged myself down to the bedroom.

In silence, we stripped down and crawled between the

sheets, and as I closed my eyes, he rolled me to my side, curling his body around mine with a contented sigh.

I was in so much trouble with this man.

NINETEEN

Cian

BLAIR WAS ACTING STRANGELY, and I didn't know what was wrong.

We'd continued the trend of trading off nights at each other's houses, the sex was off the charts hot, and I was more convinced than ever that I had to find a way to convince her to be mine, but there were moments when she got quiet. She retreated so far into herself that I couldn't follow.

Worse, the way she looked at me when she came back made me feel like I was the problem.

Not the upcoming Thanksgiving dinner, not her heavy workload that was getting bigger as Dante gave her more responsibilities, but me.

What the fuck did I do?

I'd considered throwing myself at Mia's mercy again, but I was an adult who could solve my own adult problems.

By avoiding them and hoping like hell it didn't blow up in my face.

I strolled through the halls of the shelter until I reached Seelie's cage and stopped in shock.

My dog was at the door waiting for me.

"Hey, girl."

Lowering myself slowly to my haunches, I held my hand out for her to sniff, and was rewarded with a lick.

"We've been showing her footage of you from your social page. All the little videos and photos you post, but she likes the aftergame interviews the best. She cocks her head and tries to work out how to get your attention while you talk to the camera." Katie grinned broadly at me. "It was my idea."

"Great job," I said, stunned as I offered her my knuckles for a pound.

"She still doesn't like other people, but she seems to know the days you're coming. She eats more, and spends time out of her blankets like she's waiting for you."

I narrowed my eyes on the teen as I opened the cage and stepped inside.

"You know I can't take her home with me. It's not fair to her."

She rolled her eyes, conveying my idiocy in the way only a teen girl could. "You already own her. You just don't know it yet. Sort your shit out, old man."

"Katie—"

"That's cap." She walked away, waving carelessly over her shoulder.

"I'd take you home in a heartbeat if I thought I could," I told Seelie as she waited patiently for me to sit, then curled up against my leg.

"Besides, I have enough girl troubles without adding

you in the mix." I met her beautiful brown eyes. "No offense."

Her tail thumped a couple of times against the concrete floor. It was cold under my ass. The tin wall bit into my back, and I could touch the other side without pointing my toes.

This was no place for a dog long term either.

And that was what was in store for Seelie. Unless someone else put in the same work I had and won her trust.

The thought soured my gut.

As much as it seemed completely out of reach, I'd had a vision of my future that included Seelie sleeping on the couch and Blair in my bed.

Permanently.

The sense of peace that crept over me as I entertained the fantasy again was a siren song that would lead to misery in the long run because I couldn't figure out how to keep Seelie, and I had the feeling Blair was somehow slipping through my fingers too.

The obvious answer was to ask her about it, but each time I tried, despite our promises to be honest with each other, she somehow redirected the conversation to other things.

Maybe I was being paranoid.

She hated her family, and the dinner was approaching like a freight train.

I'd wait until the dust settled on that disaster waiting to happen and then find out where things lay.

~

Blair was deep in thought as she let herself into my house that afternoon, her face fierce as she seemed to be in a mental battle of some sort.

"How was therapy?" I asked from the sofa where I'd been trying to concentrate on Wayne Gretsky's autobiography for the previous hour. I wished I could be an audiobook guy, but I couldn't concentrate well enough when I just listened.

There was a rustle and thump as her bag and keys hit the dining table, and then she was crawling into my lap. She tucked herself under my chin and heaved a sigh as I wound my arms around her.

"You scare the fuck out of me."

I waited for her to say more, but she still seemed to be processing her thoughts. If she weren't in my arms, I would have worried this was a breakup chat. The fact we weren't officially together didn't seem to matter in my panicky brain.

"Is this why you've been pulling away?" I asked.

Her head moved against my chest.

"Can I do anything to help you trust me?"

This time, it moved back and forward.

I tightened my grip and let the silence fill the room. She would talk when she was ready. Outside, the neighbor's dog barked, causing a chorus of responses from the houses nearby. A motorbike started down the road, the rumbling growing louder, then tapering off as they rode past our front door.

"I want to trust you. And I do. It's life that I don't trust. Because if you want me and I lose you, then what's left?"

"So would you give up before we even start?"

Her shoulders slumped further. "I don't want to."

"Good."

Silence returned, but it felt safer.

"I want to take you out tonight," I said after a while. She stirred beneath me, lifting her head so I could see her eyes.

"Where?"

"Somewhere nice. Will you go out with me?"

"People will see."

"Let them. You aren't a dirty secret. Who gives a fuck what they think?"

She pressed her lips to mine firmly, then climbed out of my lap.

"Okay. Let's go."

As much as I hated seeing her doubt herself—and me—over and over, the way she pulled herself together and kept moving was fucking incredible. She wanted to try. For us.

Which was exactly what you needed in a partner when you were used to being an afterthought, like I was.

"Oh, no. I don't have anything to wear."

I couldn't wait until the day when there wasn't a 'her house' and a 'my house', but at least this problem was easily solved.

After I'd changed into a suit and sent a heads up text, we drove the couple of streets to Oscar and Mia's place. While Mia and Blair disappeared into the bedroom, Oscar and I had a beer and shot the shit.

A feminine throat clearing pulled our attention to Mia standing in the doorway several minutes later. Her arms were crossed, and a smug grin tugged at her cheeks.

"She's ready."

I shot to my feet as Blair came around the corner and—Oh God, I was hard. She wore a form fitting cream dress that stopped mid-thigh with a neckline that perfectly framed her collarbones. Her usually wild curls had been pulled back into a fancy twist, and behind her glasses, her eyes looked bigger than normal, the toffee color standing out against the purple shadow on her lids. She'd told me she didn't wear eye makeup because she couldn't see well enough to put it on. Mia fixed that. The shy smile on her face told me she was happy with the results.

"What do you think?" Mia asked, knocking my shoulder and settling into Oscar's arms.

"It's hard to improve on perfection, but you look stunning."

Blair's cheeks reddened as she dropped her gaze to the floor. "You know? I actually feel it."

"Ow!" Oscar rubbed at his chest. A mock scowl pinched his brow as he eyed his wife. "Vicious. Next time you're excited, how about a kiss?"

"Not until we're out the door. Wait, just one thing." I pulled her hair loose, encouraging those riotous curls to settle around her head.

"Perfect. Thank you, Mia. We'll see you guys later."

While Blair was in with Mia, I'd reserved a table at Yujo, a high-end Japanese restaurant that had won just about every award there was in fine dining.

"I hope I don't get soy sauce on this dress," Blair murmured as we parked out front.

"I promise, I'll replace it if you do."

The restaurant seemed to be doing a steady business as we were shown to a table at the back as per my reservation request.

"There are people looking at us," she murmured through a tight smile as we took our seats.

"They don't matter. Focus on me."

By the time our meals arrived, she had forgotten about everyone else in the restaurant.

"No way could Crosby have beaten Messier," she shouted, outrage written across her face. "Are you crazy?"

I chuckled and held out my hands.

She huffed, flopping back into her seat dramatically. "I don't think I can be on this date anymore."

I grinned at her as the waiter brought over new plates. "Not even if I bribe you with mochi?"

"I'll allow it," she teased with a roll of her eyes. She bit into the pillowy dessert with a sigh, a private smile tipping up her lips. This had been a great idea.

"I've had a lot of fun tonight," I told her as I reached for a second mochi. These things were amazing.

"Me too."

Under the dim lights of the restaurant, she glowed with a kind of confidence I prayed would still be there in the morning.

The only thing I knew for sure was that I'd be the guy lucky enough to be there to see it.

CHAPTER
TWENTY

Blair

MY SKIN WAS HOT. Zings of pleasure zipped through my veins as I moaned, sliding a leg up over the sheets to give deeper access to the body on top of me. Without bothering to open my eyes, I arched my back, making room for the hand that slipped between my belly and the sheets and worked its way down to stroke lazy circles over my clit.

"Mmmm, morning," I drawled.

He bit my shoulder lightly, his hips sliding back until just his head was still inside, then filled me again in a long stroke.

"I love waking up inside you. Love having you when you're all warm and sleepy."

He hummed, the vibration tunneling into my ear and fueling the arousal that flowed through me like warm honey.

His fingers stroked down my pussy until they framed the point at which we were joined.

"You feel so good stretched around my dick. We fit so perfectly."

He rained kisses over my hairline and jaw until I turned into him, letting him take control of my mouth as his hips moved with more urgency.

When he'd first suggested we try cock warming, I'd had to Google the term. Then I'd been worried he wouldn't be able to fall asleep with an erection, but I loved it. Having him wrapped around me, inside me, as we slept, made me feel safe and cared for in a way I never knew I needed.

The wakeup sex was a great way to start the day, too.

I gasped into the pillows as the slapping sounds of our bodies filled the quiet space.

"Time to come for me, baby. I want you to finish before me."

Like he'd trained me at some point in the last two weeks, the orgasm flooded through my body on a wave of pleasure. I released a sound somewhere between keening and a sigh as my body tightened around him.

A few strokes later, Cian dropped his forehead between my shoulder blades, shuddering through his own release. He pulled out of me slowly and tapped my thigh.

"Open."

Since we'd had the birth control/safe sex discussion, we'd given up condoms and I'd learned just how much of a caveman Cian was.

Sliding one knee up the bed, I grinned at his groan of appreciation. His fingers stroked over my sensitive flesh, working his cum over my pussy lips and pushing it back inside so he could watch it drip back out.

"So fucking sexy," he breathed. With fingertips covered in his release, he worked my pussy until he pulled a second orgasm from me before leaving to start the shower.

When he returned, he paused in the doorway and took in my disheveled state.

"New plan. Screw Thanksgiving, we're staying here so you can look like that for the rest of the day."

I chuckled and gathered my strength to get upright.

"I'd love to, but I'm going shopping with Mia for tonight. We can't let the orphans down."

He grumbled, but faithfully followed me into the shower.

I rewarded him by getting on my knees before we got out.

He was right. His hot water system was far superior to mine.

"Good turnout tonight," Dante muttered beside me as we watched players and the who's who of Austin mingle over drinks while waiting for dinner to be served.

"Hopefully, they'll raise a decent amount to donate. Do we know if they're doing a silent auction again this year?"

Dante hummed, looking out over the crowd like someone might fuck things up if she let her guard down. In the corner of the room, Silas Johannsen, one of our first line defensemen, stood with a beer in hand and scowl on face, daring any of the reporters present to try to talk to him. Beside him, our goalie, Keaton Constantine, stood in a slouch that radiated sexual tension. Those two were trouble, if they chose to be. Dante's eyes returned to them, but she seemed to assess them as low risk and turned her attention back to me.

"So how are you feeling about everything?"

I opened my mouth, ready to tell her all about how well

Cian and I had been getting along when I realized she meant the job.

"It's a steep learning curve, but I feel like I'm getting the hang of a lot of it. Are you sure you don't want to stick around for another season before I take the training wheels off and apply? They'll probably find a better candidate if they open up the interviews."

"Blair."

The look she shot me spoke volumes.

I sighed. She was right. I'd kept her updated on my therapy sessions, and she seemed genuinely happy to hear the progress I was making.

Confidence is the most important part of the job, she'd told me time and again. And while sometimes I felt more like I was running with *fake it 'til you make it*, I had promised myself I would, in fact, try to 'make it'.

We took our seats shortly after and, much to Cian's annoyance, our allocated seating had us on different tables.

My phone buzzed as our starters were served and I grinned at the sight of his name.

Cian: You're too far away. Switch seats

You'll survive. Eat your food

Cian: I'd rather eat you *wink face*

Behave, and you can later

I put my phone down and tried to engage in the conversation around me. Remy was talking to Dante about a charity idea for the team.

"Are you talking about Austin Animal Allies?" I broke in at the mention of a shelter.

"Yeah, have you heard of it?"

I nodded. "Yeah, I've been there before. It's a really great space, and the animals are well cared for."

He gave me a smile of acknowledgment and turned back to Dante to continue his pitch.

"They have a few different locations around the city. It'd be really cool to support them to upgrade some of the older facilities."

My phone buzzed again. I opened the chat, then slammed the device face down on the table, my cheeks radiating heat. Cian's chair was empty at the other table. Of course. Because you couldn't take a photo like that in company.

I slid my phone into my lap, ensuring my table mates wouldn't be able to see, and tapped out a reply.

> You're missing your meal

> Cian: I'll eat later. Play with me.

I scrolled up to the photo he'd sent and my belly swooped with arousal. Wherever he was, the lighting wasn't the best, but I could still make out the vein I liked to run my tongue down, as well as his swollen purple head. The low light glistened off a bead of precum on his tip, and I wondered if he was taking care of things himself while I sat with his teammates.

> Blair: What do you want me to do?

> Cian: Part your thighs and take a photo up that skirt of yours

Around the table, people were engaged in conversation. Some were animated, others somber as they picked at their food. I was nervous about playing the game Cian proposed, mostly because there was something he didn't know about my outfit. Sliding to the edge of my chair, I thanked whatever event coordinator had decided to use floor length tablecloths as I hid behind the folds of fabric and snapped a photo. Before I could second guess myself, I hit send and deleted the evidence from my gallery.

> Cian: WHERE THE FUCK ARE YOUR PANTIES?! Fuuuuuuuck *eggplant emoji* *squirting emoji*

I hid a smile and put my phone aside to focus on the conversation around me, praying no one questioned the flush in my cheeks.

It couldn't have been more than ten minutes later when Cian appeared at my shoulder.

"Excuse us," he said to Dante as he cupped my elbow. "I need to borrow her."

I laughed as he grabbed my bag and towed me out of the room. As soon as we were outside, he pinned me to the brick wall and took my mouth in a fiery kiss.

His hands roamed across my breasts and down over my ass, fingertips tracing the crack and making me shudder.

"We're supposed to be inside," I gasped as he teased the hem of my dress. "And Dante will kill us both if we get caught and cause a sex scandal."

"Worth it," he muttered as he mouthed his way along my collarbone. I groaned and pushed at his pecs, not wanting to stop, but knowing we needed to.

"Your truck."

He glanced up, brow furrowed for a moment before he clearly came to the same conclusion I did. He'd parked at the back of the lot where it would be difficult for attendees to see.

Hand in hand, we all but ran toward his ride and dove into the back seat. As I slammed the door, he worked his buckle, pushing his pants and boxers off his hips and pulling me over him. My skirt rode up as I positioned him beneath me and sat down hard, pulling a lusty sigh from both of us.

"You're turning me into a sex fiend with your magic dick," I said, grinding against him.

"You always were, you just needed the right person to bring it out in you."

I slapped his chest and he caught my hands, wrapping them behind my back as he pushed up into me. His pubic bone rubbed against my clit in this position, and I dropped my forehead to his shoulder, panting as sparks flew through my body.

"Come on, baby, give it to me." He was all around me. His arms wrapped me tightly as his breath coasted over my ear. He bit my lobe, and I came with a curse on a shuddering breath.

As usual, he rode out my orgasm before giving into his own, and when we were both floating in post-orgasmic bliss, he reached into his pants pocket for a handful of tissues.

"I stole them from the restrooms after you sent me that picture," he said by way of explanation as he cleaned me with gentle wipes. "You have no idea how much I want to take you back inside with my cum dripping down your legs, but I'll just have to make do with the knowledge that we'll be doing that again as soon as we get home."

I kissed him sweetly as he continued to clean me up,

marveling at how someone could be so considerate and so dirty all at once. I loved all the facets of Cian O'Leary.

And that thought didn't scare me anywhere near as much as it used to.

CHAPTER
TWENTY-ONE

Cian

"Nice flow, Disney Princess," Colorado's left defenseman, Aiden Fowler, jeered as he took me into the boards for the third freaking time this period. The asshole was a friend of Chet Doyle, and didn't that say everything about his character. He'd been at me all game, but since I'd already managed to score a goal and an assist, and Constantine hadn't let through a single puck, it was easier to keep my cool. I wasn't aiming for a Gordie Howe hat trick tonight. I had plans with Blair after the game to distract her from thoughts of tomorrow.

"Maybe pay a little less attention to me, and a little more to Parry. He's a sieve tonight. You may as well warm up the bus."

Fowler growled, and I used his distraction to send the biscuit down the guts of the ice to Miller. The crowd screamed "It's Miller Time!" as he lined up his shot, and I shoved Fowler off me with a nasty grin.

"Distraction will cost you."

I moved to the middle of the ice to intercept the puck as Parry finally managed to block a shot.

Nothing beat the thrill of playing in front of a home crowd. The cheers of the fans echoed through the barn, amping up the adrenaline, and forcing us to skate faster, shoot harder. The cold air bit at my cheeks as I skated across the red line, determined to put another point on the board before we headed to the locker room.

Fowler was hard on my ass as I chased down the puck, and as I stretched my stick out to pull it in, the world fell off kilter. My skate stopped and my body overbalanced. I was moving too fast, and the corner of the rink where the boards met the ice rose to meet my face. A crack shuddered through my body, but there was no time for panic.

Just darkness.

I came to as my body was rolled face up and lifted. Oh, I was on a stretcher. When had that happened?

Oscar's concerned face hovered over me, but when I tried to turn my head, it wouldn't move.

"You have a brace on, just chill here, my man. They're going to get you checked out by the doc."

He grasped my hand, and I wondered what happened to my gloves.

The crowd screamed their support as I was carted off the ice.

"What happened?"

"Fucking Fowler tripped you, the dirty piece of shit." Oscar didn't let much bother him, but he was loyal to a fault. No one messed with his people.

"Go back out there and win this thing. Tell the team no retaliation."

"You have a concussion. You don't know what you're saying."

"Come on, Caveman. We don't play dirty. Don't sink to their level."

He hummed, a deep frown creasing his brow, but I knew he'd listen. As soon as we got to the medical suite, he peeled off and headed back to the locker room while I was poked and prodded.

Concussion was the diagnosis.

"You're out for the next three games, then we'll review. Rest for the next twenty-four hours, then light exercise until you see me. Any concerns, call me immediately," Dr. Preston said, leaning against the bed with his arms folded. "No, we're not compromising. No, there's nothing you can do to speed up the process except rest. Needless to say, you aren't going back out there tonight, so get comfortable. If you want a shower, it has to be lukewarm and make sure someone is there in case you lose consciousness again."

I grumbled at the instructions, hating that he was so seasoned he didn't even pretend to let me argue the facts.

"There's a very concerned social media manager outside the door. I'll leave you with her while I restock the Tylenol."

He ducked out, murmuring to a pale-faced Blair who barely acknowledged him.

"Holy shit, I thought you were dead." Her voice wavered as she rushed into my arms, body shaking as I held her tightly.

"I'm fine."

She pulled back and pinned me with a hard look. "You're not fine. You lost consciousness. God, you hit the boards and just flopped like a rag doll."

Her eyes shone behind her glasses. I tried to pull her in again, and she punched me in the arm.

"Don't ever scare me like that again!"

"I'll try."

She snuggled back into me, apparently forgiving me for my thoughtless actions.

Her warm body distracted me from the dull thud in my skull, and I breathed a heavy sigh, relaxing into the contact.

She always made me feel better.

"We should call your parents and let them know you're all right," she said after a while.

"I don't think they'll care," I said. At her look, I shrugged. "Go ahead, though."

I recited the number and she put the phone on speaker as it rang.

"Hello?" No matter what my mom was saying, she always sounded rushed to my ears. As though she couldn't stand to spend time on things she considered beneath her.

"Hello, Mrs. O'Leary?"

"Who's this?"

"My name's Blair, I work with the Aces. I wanted to get in touch in case you were watching the game tonight. I have Cian here, and I just wanted to let you know that he's okay."

There was silence on the other end of the line. Blair tilted the phone to check the call was still connected, but after a moment, my mother spoke, sounding harried.

"Look, I don't know why you're calling us. Cian can get himself out of whatever he's done. The boy was always needy, but he's an adult now and we have more important things going on here. Please don't call again."

Blair stared in shock as the call dropped. Shame burned

through me. I didn't want her to know about this side of me.

Deep down, I was still the kid who wanted his parents to care, but reality was what it was, and I had managed to keep myself alive this long. It was only when I'd started this thing with Blair that I realized just how much I needed someone there. I'd overcompensated for a lot of years by being that person for everyone else, but Oscar and Mia had been my only support system for a long time.

Now I had Blair.

"I'm sorry, I didn't realize," she said quietly, pocketing her phone, as though it could hide the conversation she'd just had.

"It's okay."

"No. It's not. But that's not on you."

I gave her a small smile and dragged her into my arms to hold her just a bit longer.

"I'm not allowed to play the rest of the game. Or the rest of the week. Shit, I wonder if he'll bench me for the Vegas game."

Blair put a soft hand over my mouth.

"How about we take this one day at a time. Don't start with the *what-ifs* or you'll drive yourself mad."

"Therapy's really helping, huh?" I asked against her palm. She replaced it with her lips for a swift kiss, then stood back.

"I have to get back for the last period, but do you need anything?"

I shook my head. "Just you when you're done. I'll meet you at my truck."

She blew a kiss at the door and left me to my pounding head and circling thoughts.

TWENTY-TWO

Blair

"Are you ready?"

"Yes." No.

I didn't want to subject Cian to my family, especially after learning that his was just as bad, possibly worse, the night before, but the thought of facing them on my own made me want to vomit. More than once on the drive here, I'd caught him wincing, but he'd refused to let me drive, and insisted he didn't need medication. He was here for me completely.

I used the door knocker, striking the wood three times only, because heaven forbid I exceed what was polite and be viewed as harassing the occupants. A joyful bark echoed through the door, and I allowed myself a small smile at the only light in visiting my parents.

The door opened, letting out a waft of tomatoes, flour, and tobacco as a five-foot-nothing nightmare appeared in a black dress and frilly apron.

"Blair, so nice of you to join us." Her voice was like ice, as cold and unmoved as her forehead since she'd started investing in botox.

"Hi Mom," I muttered, subtly squeezing Cian's hand and receiving a squeeze in return.

"And who's this?" Her eyes traced over my date. Evaluating him and finding him wanting purely because he kept company with me.

"Nice to meet you, ma'am, I'm Cian." He held his hand out for a shake and received a sniff in return. Without another word, she turned back into the house, leaving the door open behind her.

"Leave your shoes at the door," she said over her shoulder as she opened the door into the kitchen. A bang and crash sounded as a mop-haired dog muscled through the gap and barreled down the hall.

"Get ready. This is the only fun we'll have today."

I didn't bother to explain as I lay flat on my back and let the golden retriever crawl all over me in greeting. Bessie was the youngest in a long line of retrievers my parents had owned, dutifully returning to the same breeder whenever the last one passed on. When Georgia and I were younger— before we'd declared ourselves mortal enemies—we'd made a tradition of greeting the dog like this whenever we got home from school.

I giggled as Bessie slipped and slid over me, her tongue knocking my glasses askew and her foot punching into my gut, knocking the wind out of me.

"This seems hazardous," Cian said with a laugh, hooking me under the arms to pull me to my feet.

"Fun though." I grinned at him as he scrubbed his hands through the mountains of fur.

"She's beautiful," he said, a sad look flitting across his face.

Damn it, he was thinking about his parents.

I was so mad at them. How could they not see that Cian was one of the best people in the world?

How could they know him and not love him?

"Come on." I took his hand and led him through the house to the back deck where Dad was chatting animatedly with a long-haired blond man, while Miss Perfect herself sat beside him picking at her nails. This must be the boyfriend.

"Holy shit! Cian O'Leary!" Dad burst out of his chair in a rush, his hand leading the way for a firm shake. "What are you doing here? Duckie, you didn't tell me you were bringing Cian O'Leary to the house. How's the head, son? That was one hell of a knock you took last night."

Cian looked slightly overwhelmed, but took it well.

"Nothing a little rest won't fix. It's good to meet you, sir."

Dad took Cian by the elbow, leading him to the table and pulling out the chair beside him. With nothing else to do, I grabbed a couple of sodas from the bar fridge and joined them.

The blond guy offered me a smile as I sat beside Cian.

"Hi, I'm Weston."

"Blair," I said, flicking a glance at Georgia.

"How much did you have to pay him to come here?" she asked in lieu of a greeting. Great. Nothing had changed since we last spoke. Still a bitch.

"I didn't."

She snorted, rolling her eyes as she sat back with her wine glass. Weston glanced between us, a small frown creasing his brow.

"Oh! Hey, you play for the Engines, right?" I asked as the answer to where I'd seen his face before suddenly hit me.

"Yeah, I do. I play tight end. Do you watch?"

"Whenever I can, the hockey season keeps me busy though."

"That's sport, isn't it?" We shared a knowing smile, and I ignored the dark cloud beside him. How the hell did such a nice guy get sucked in by the likes of her?

Mom brought out the appetizers, and Cian slid a hand over my knee as she joked he should "Blink twice" if he was being held against his will. I gritted my teeth against a retort as my family echoed the words of internet trolls who had never met me.

Wasn't family supposed to support each other?

I looked across at Georgia, so perfectly put together with her designer clothing, her immaculate makeup and size zero waist. She picked at her appetizer half-heartedly, and barely touched her entrée as Mom swapped the plates over.

When was the last time we had been comfortable in each other's company? Let alone friendly.

Not since we hit puberty. Maybe not before.

"Hey, Cian. Do you know why Blair is called Duckie? Tell him, Blair. It's funny. It's because she's the ugly duckling. Get it?"

Maybe never.

She scooped some potatoes from the bowl in the center of the table and, predictably, Mom clicked her tongue.

"Do you really need that, Georgia? You won't keep your job long if you stack on more weight."

Weston and Cian looked between Georgia and Mom, their mouths slightly open in horror.

This is my family, I wanted to tell them. *Run while you still have a chance.*

Instead, we all ate in silence until Mom put her cutlery down with a sigh.

"It really was nice of you to be here with Blair today, but I can't in good conscience let you get her hopes up. If this is transactional, that's fine, but if not... this is just cruel."

"What...do you mean?" Cian asked, his grip tightening on my knee.

"Well, all I'm saying is that if you expect us to believe that an athlete like you would be interested in someone like her, then clearly something else is going on. I don't like deception and I'd hate to think you were using her."

I'd never understood what I did to make her hate me. There must have been a time when I was little that she'd acted like a proper mother, but I didn't remember it. Maybe she'd taken one look at me after birth and decided I was a lost cause.

"That's enough."

His voice was low but powerful as he looked around the table.

"None of you appreciate this woman, and I'm not going to let her sit here and listen to you belittle her anymore."

"You're telling me you're not just pretending to date her? Yeah, right." Georgia sniffed, doing a double take as she noticed the look on Weston's face.

"There's nothing pretend about how I feel for Blair. You don't deserve her. None of you. We're leaving now, and Blair will decide if she ever speaks to any of you again. In case you can't tell, I'll be advising her against it unless you pull your heads out of your asses. Weston, it was genuinely nice to meet you."

Cian's hand was gentle as he pulled me out of my seat

and escorted me through the house and out to his truck.

We pulled away from the old Victorian building with a squeal of tires and turned toward home. There was no sound in the cab except for the white noise of the tires on the road for several miles, both of us stuck in our own heads as we processed the scene we just left. I glanced at his profile, so proud, still so full of righteous fury and felt a bubbling in my chest.

It forced its way out of my throat in a laugh that took both of us by surprise. Once the dam broke, we were both lost, to the point Cian pulled over to avoid colliding with a parked car.

"Oh, my God. That was so freaking dope! I can't believe you scolded my whole family. You're amazing."

His cheeks were ruddy as he turned to face me.

"I don't even know why I'm laughing right now. I was so mad. I wanted to punch your mom, and I'd never hit a woman."

"She's an asshole." I sighed.

"They all are."

"Well, not Weston. He seemed genuinely appalled at their behavior. I don't know why he's spending time with Georgia, but good luck to him. He'll need it."

Cian reached across and threaded his fingers through mine.

"I didn't know about the Duckie thing."

Of course he didn't. Cian didn't have a mean bone in his body, and that was why it hit different.

"I know. I don't mind when you call me that."

He grunted, squeezing my hand in acknowledgment before he changed the subject to more important things.

"Coffee?"

"Hell yes. We deserve it."

CHAPTER
TWENTY-THREE

Cian

I SURVIVED my forced rest period, despite having to sit out three away games in a row, which meant Blair traveled with the team while I was stuck at home. My first game back, we beat Calgary at home and had a quiet celebration afterward. Just the two of us.

Blair's family hadn't tried to reach out, thank God. I'd meant what I said, and I tensed up, ready for action anytime her phone rang.

Tonight, she was leaving her phone at home, though, because the Aces were having their Christmas party, and I'd convinced Blair to go as my date.

Officially.

No more bullshit friends with benefits.

She was already at Oscar and Mia's getting ready while I got some bits and pieces sorted for our own private Christmas party the following week. I loved how easily my friends had accepted her into our little chosen family, and I knew that Mia loved Blair for Blair, not just who she was to me. She'd threatened me with bodily harm if I fucked things up the week before and all but told me Blair would get her in the breakup, and by extension Oscar. I knew she was joking, kind of, but it still reminded me how important it was for me to get this right.

"Did you get your tree done?" Oscar asked as I stepped into a cloud of cinnamon and clove scented heaven.

"Yeah, I did. Why does it smell so good in here?"

"Mia found the Christmas candles. The girls are just about ready." He handed me a beer and settled back against the kitchen counter.

"So... I have to tell you something."

His eyes were wary, a look I couldn't ever remember seeing on my best friend's face before.

"What's up? And how can I help?"

He shook his head. "Nah, nothing like that, but it's going to change things."

Their doorbell chimed, announcing the arrival of the limo we'd hired, but I kept my gaze locked on my friend.

He sighed, raking his hand through his hair and scrubbing his face.

"Mmff frefrowow."

"In English?" I asked.

"Mia's pregnant."

Joy rushed through my body as I threw my arms around him with a shout.

"Holy shit! Congratulations, man. Wait... this is good news, right?"

Oscar relaxed, returning the hug with a solid back slap.

"Oh, yeah. We've been... not trying, but not... not trying? If you get what I mean. We wanted to sort of leave it to fate, but now it's happened and I guess we're both freaking out a bit."

"That's amazing. I'm going to have to start planning ways to beat out Luca for favorite uncle."

Mia's brother was a surly, touch averse, mean bastard... who was going to love this kid like his life depended on it.

Oscar huffed a laugh and took a long pull on his drink as the click of matching sets of heels echoed down the hall.

Oscar whistled while I tried to remember how to breathe as our women stepped through the doorway and came in for hugs.

"You told him?" Mia asked. I snatched her into a quick hug on her way past as Oscar growled good-naturedly.

"Congratulations, Mumma," I whispered, letting her go to her man as Blair stepped in to take her place.

"Hey, you." She tilted her head back, and I touched my lips to hers in a gentle kiss that wouldn't mess up her lipstick.

"Time to go," Oscar announced.

We all piled into the limo and drank soda in deference to Mia on the ride in.

The room was already packed as we wandered in, music playing over speakers hidden behind tinsel and mistletoe. On one side of the room was a table full of items to be auctioned off for charity, while the bar was on the other.

"Can I get you a drink?" I asked Blair, running my hand down her back. The dress exposed all of the soft skin between the nape of her neck and her lower back. I couldn't stop touching her and already had plans for when I could get it off her. She asked for a white wine and I wasted no time getting her order along with beers for me and Oscar, and sparkling water for Mia.

"Check it out," I murmured to her as she sipped her wine. "Mistletoe."

She smiled and lifted her chin.

Carding my hands through her hair, I pulled her mouth to mine in a kiss that was still semi fit for the public, but left no doubt about what would come later.

"Holy shit. You work fast, O'Leary. Looks like I owe you fifty bucks."

The obnoxious voice broke through my happy moment, and I couldn't suppress a low growl as Chet fucking Doyle muscled his way into our space.

"Look at her, she's panting like the dog she is. You only had to bang her. Seducing her is above and beyond, brother. You are stone cold."

Blair's body was stiff beneath my hands, and I didn't know if it would make things better or worse if I cold cocked this son of a bitch to shut him the hell up.

I'd probably get some kind of community service medal for improving the culture in the Aces organization.

His laugh was a vile taunt intended to tear Blair down the same way her family had tried, but there was no fucking way I'd let that happen.

"Shut the fuck up, Doyle."

"No, no. You deserve all the accolades here. I've witnessed a master at work. Did you get her to tell you she loved you? Fuck, yes. You're a straight up killer."

Blair broke out of my hold and headed for the door while Chet's laughter nipped at her heels.

Stay and break his face? Or chase down the woman I was in love with.

Violence sounded like such an easy answer, but at the end of the day he was irrelevant.

Blair mattered.

Spinning on my heel, I chased after her, heels skidding to a halt when I found her leaning against the wall outside.

"Wait... what? Ahh, I can explain."

"I know you can. And you will." Her voice was calm. Not in a shut down, dissociating way, but a *what idiocy did you pull? Tell me so I can help* way.

"During preseason, he was being an asshole."

"Standard."

"And he started ranting about this stupid idea for a bet."

She nodded, waiting for me to continue.

"Anyway, he wouldn't shut the fuck up, so I said yes so you wouldn't have to walk in and hear all the shit he was spewing. I'd forgotten about it until he said it just then. It was stupid, and I didn't get to know you for the money. I'm in love with you. Plus, Mia's already picked your side if we break up and I can't lose my friends."

She was too calm. As she leaned against the wall with a foot cocked, arms folded across the front of her sinful dress, I wanted to fall to my knees and prove how much she meant to me.

But I'd also just said I loved her, and she wasn't reacting to that either.

"That was pretty stupid," she said eventually, and my heart let out a hard thump in relief.

"It was."

"But your heart was in the right place."

"You're taking this really well." I held both hands out. "Not that I'm complaining, just observing that you are."

She smirked as she stepped into my body and wound her arms around my neck.

"It's pretty easy when you told me you loved me weeks ago."

"What?" I pulled back, searching her face for signs she was joking. I would remember telling her I loved her, right?

"After the Boston game. You passed out in the car on the drive home, and when I tried to wake you, you told me then."

I screwed up my face, trying to remember the night. There was a vague memory of Wyatt kissing his girlfriend, and some filthy ideas I'd since put into practice with Blair, but nothing between O'Malley's and waking up the next morning.

But something else occurred to me.

"Is that why you pulled away from me?"

She fidgeted with her skirt.

"It took some time, and some conversations with my therapist to process what you'd said. My old way of thinking kept looking to disprove it, but I wanted it to be real so badly that I couldn't cut and run like I thought I had to."

It made sense. Safety didn't seem so safe when you were used to the chaos. A whole paradigm shift was needed to be able to recognize our worth.

"Would it help if I said it again?" I asked, running my hands over her back because I could.

"Maybe." she tilted her head, a playful smile pulling at her perfect lips.

"I love you, Blair Kennedy."

A beautiful pink flushed up her cheeks as I licked at her smile, asking her to let me in. She opened up to me and I took her mouth in a kiss that was all about possession. She was mine. Now. Forever.

"Just so you know, we're officially ditching this friends with benefits thing," I growled.

Blair hummed.

"You are my girlfriend, and one day soon, you'll be my fiancée. I don't want you to doubt what my intentions are here."

"Getting a bit ahead of yourself, aren't you? I think we'll have to talk about the benefits package," she drawled, surprising a laugh out of me.

I bent my head back toward her and just before we kissed, she murmured, "I love you," against my lips.

EPILOGUE

Cian

Six months later

Our season ended in May when the Richland Renegades knocked the Aces out during the second round of the playoffs. The team was disappointed, but already talking training plans for the coming season, including new trades and sourcing some promising rookies.

I'd just broken down another cardboard box when the sound of keys in the door caught my attention. Blair burst inside, raced across the room and threw herself at me, knowing I'd always catch her. Wrapping her legs around my waist, she covered my face in kisses as I walked us over to the sofa.

"Good news?" I guessed, sitting down with her straddling my lap.

"I got the job! Dante's going to keep training me for

now, and I'll be your official PR manager come the first game of preseason."

I kissed her hard, trying to convey how fucking proud of her I was. She'd worked her ass off to get here, and it made me so happy to see my team recognize how much she deserved it.

She looked over my shoulder, taking in the room around us.

"You've been busy."

When Blair's lease came up for renewal last month, we decided it wasn't worth keeping two houses, and seeing as we spent more time here, we decided she'd move in with me. While she was blowing away my team's executives, I'd been unpacking boxes to remove the trip hazards around the house. Plus, I wanted her settled so she couldn't change her mind.

"Yup." I stretched my arms along the back of the sofa, loving the feeling of her squirming with excitement on my lap. And completely unrepentant about the erection straining at my hips.

"Insatiable," she muttered with a grin, sliding off the sofa to position herself between my knees.

"With you? Always." I lifted my hips as she slid my sweatpants to my ankles, then ran her tongue up my shaft. She sucked my head between her lips and took me all the way to the back of her throat, humming as she bobbed over me. When she started to squirm, I pulled her up, waving off her noise of protest as I stripped her pants from her legs and lay along the couch.

"I'm not stopping you, I want you to ride my face."

She pecked a kiss on my lips before following instructions as beautifully as usual. She swung a leg over my head, lowering her hips until I could bury my tongue in her sweet pussy and went right back to playing with my balls as she mouthed at my shaft. Her lavender and honey scent filled my nose as she rocked against my tongue, her mouth becoming more and more enthusiastic as she lost herself in the sensation. I looped an arm around her leg and pushed two fingers deep into her core, giving her something to push back on as I flattened my tongue and lapped at her clit. Her moan vibrated through my balls, making them pull tight against my body. Fuck, the view, the taste, the smell, all of it conspired against me as her hot mouth took me all the way inside again. Adding a third finger, I worked to get her there first, but lost the battle as she scraped her teeth along my length. I came with a curse, my hips bucking uncontrollably as she swallowed through the aftershocks. As soon as I settled, I turned her around so she could fuck my face until she covered me with her juices.

I licked my lips as she shuffled down my body, curling against my side with a contented sigh.

"How are you feeling? I asked.

"Sleepy. I'll get up in a minute, though, otherwise we'll be late."

I hummed in agreement. Our appointment was the only thing that could have made me want to leave the house after a session like that. Even still, there was a part of me that wanted to postpone and take Blair upstairs to drag another half dozen orgasms from her.

I could never get enough. Which was why I had something burning a hole in my pocket that, in retrospect, I was glad she hadn't noticed when she stripped me before.

Was it tacky to propose after sex? Definitely.

I should wait.

Maybe take her back to that Japanese restaurant she liked.

"Marry me."

Shit.

"What?"

"When we tell this story in the future, we can pretend I did it in some romantic way, and not half naked on the sofa with your pussy juices drying on my face, but I have no filter around you. Marry me. Please."

"If I say yes now, will you give me a redo so there's a safe for work version of this story?"

My body shook with the urge to laugh.

"Definitely."

"Then yes. Pending a better story." She pulled me into a kiss, then sat up, slapping my thigh a little too close to my balls for comfort.

"Come on. Let's get changed and head out."

The Austin Animal Allies shelter looked the same as always, which felt a little weird considering the life-changing decisions that had happened already today.

The round cut diamond that Mia helped me buy sparkled on Blair's hand where it sat in mine, and I couldn't stop looking at it.

She'd agreed to marry me.

And we were about to complete our little family.

I'd spent time thinking about how Katie had comforted Seelie with footage of me, and floated the idea with the shelter of providing videos of Blair, Oscar, and Mia, so she could become used to them, too. We'd experimented over the last couple of weeks first with Blair, then Oscar, then finally Mia with a very anxious Oscar hovering nearby. Mia's belly was round as a basketball, and Seelie had laid her head against it, like she could hear the baby inside.

Our little found family had all agreed to help with the

care of Seelie, so she'd never be alone, and Katie had offered to dog sit if Mia needed a break while we were away.

At the end of the row, the cage rattled and Seelie emerged wearing a halter and led by Katie. I accepted the lead and took my girls outside, getting Seelie situated in the crate we'd trained her to use, and headed home.

Oscar and Mia were planning to meet us later for dinner to officially meet Seelie in her new home and celebrate our engagement.

Blair wanted me to edit our engagement story already, but they'd know.

Family always knew.

I laced my fingers through hers and raised her fist to my mouth as we steered through the streets of Austin.

I had my sport, my dog, and my woman.

Luckiest guy ever.

Thank you so much for reading!

I hope you loved Cian and Blair's story as much as I do!

Are you curious about Blair's sister, Gia, and Weston the football player? You can read their story in False Start today.

IF YOU'RE interested in seeing where Oscar and Mia started, check out Kicking it with the Winger, out now!

SIGN up for TL's newsletter to find out about new books!

NEXT UP IN the Austin Aces Hockey Club series is Tripped Up by Allie Lasky. Read on for an exclusive first look...

TRIPPED UP BY ALLIE LASKY

Chapter 1 - Elsy

Surrounded by a million boxes, I look around the tiny, cluttered apartment and sigh.

"It's not that bad," Bex says. She helped drive my U-Haul from Boston to Austin. I don't know what I'm going to do without her.

It took us four days to drive across the country. Despite living together for three years and being friends for two more, I think those four days might have permanently damaged our friendship.

I feel bad for leaving, even though I knew it was the right thing for me.

We met in grad school at Stanford, keeping in touch over the years, and when I accepted the Boston Symphony contract two years ago, it made sense for me to move in with her and her roommate, Vanessa. She had an extra room. I needed a place to stay. It was perfect.

The trio of us became a tightly knit trio in our few short years together. I'm going to miss them. A lot.

When things went south for me in Boston, I knew I had to get out, and fast. It was only a few weeks later that I packed up all my things and drove across the country.

Austin will be a fresh start. I need it.

There's a knock on my door and, curious, I open it. I'm not expecting anyone. The property manager already came by. Maybe this is a friendly neighbor? Hopefully, they'll be my age and single.

A tall, built, light-haired man stands on my doorstep. Wyatt Whitney, professional hockey player and the bane of my existence, props an arm on the doorframe and scowls.

"Elsabeth."

"What are you doing here?" I snap.

He arches an eyebrow. "That's how you thank me?"

My laugh is bitter. "Thank you for what?"

"I invited him over," Bex calls from behind me. "Come on in, Wy."

I glare at her. "Why's he here?"

"Because you have ten thousand boxes and I want to get you unpacked sometime before next year," she says with a grin. "By the time I board that plane tomorrow, I want to be confident you're not going to starve or break your neck tripped up over boxes."

It's only then that I see Wyatt holding a toolbox, a bag of takeout in his other hand.

It's not my best friend's fault that I hate her brother. She doesn't know I slept with him—years before I knew they were related.

It is his fault that he doesn't remember we hooked up. He's always treated me like I'm nothing more than the scum on his shoes.

And yeah, I know it was only ever supposed to be a one-night stand, but for him not to remember me after?

My best friend Mitch invited me to go with him to Ottawa for the World Juniors championship and took me to a bar to hang out with his hockey buddies. Wyatt came up and flirted with me, obviously trying to steal me away from Mitch. It's never been like that with us; we've always been strictly platonic, but he didn't know that.

He was cute; I was drunk and lonely, so I went back to his hotel room with him. I snuck out in the morning before he woke up and went about my day.

But then I saw him in the hotel lobby with a few of the other hockey players. They were teasing him about going home with a "tubby butterface with good tits."

Hey, I was drunk, Wyatt said. At least she put out.

My stomach sank. The sweet, charming guy I'd seen glimpses of turned out to be a pig in his natural environment. What a disappointment. He was just like every other guy I'd met.

Our eyes met.

He saw my face.

He knew I heard.

And I've never been able to forget that.

I met Bex two years later, and it was another year and a half before I had a reason to meet her brother.

And when we met up in that dirty college dive bar, it was clear from the blank look on his face that he didn't remember me. He introduced himself with a disinterested handshake and immediately started hitting on another woman.

In the years since, he's always treated me like any of Bex's other friends. Distant. Sometimes cold. Never cruel. It's clear he has no idea why I dislike him, but he's always given it back just as good, so evidently it doesn't bother him.

Wyatt sets the bag of takeout on the counter. "What do you want first, building furniture or lunch?"

"Lunch. Definitely," Bex answers for us.

My stomach lurches, and it's definitely not from hunger. I don't like eating in front of him. We've only shared a few meals together over the years, and always with his sister chaperoning. It makes me remember the sick feeling in my stomach that morning all those years ago. I'm fat. I know I'm fat. I don't need it pointed out to me. Especially after a man has just had me naked in his bed.

Eating in front of him? That's a level of vulnerability I've never been able to get over. Almost as big as taking my shirt off in front of a man.

The apartment has a high counter with a bar area, but we have no stools yet, so we stand around the counter. Even though I didn't bring much furniture with me, I have enough stuff to clutter the place. It sets my teeth on edge. I don't like clutter.

That reminds me; I need to take my meds. Fishing the bottle out of my purse, I tap a tablet into my palm and wash it down with my can of Coke. The carbonation makes it not the most pleasant experience, but one I'm well used to. Water is for the weak.

Bex grabs the bag of food, handing me the tuna salad sandwich and giving Wyatt two turkey clubs, keeping the roast beef for herself. She must have told him that tuna salad is my favorite. Everyone else hates it, which just means more for me. There's even a container of potato salad. Score!

"This place is right around the corner," Wyatt says.

I arch an eyebrow. Why is he talking to me?

"I snagged their menu in case you want to order from

them again." He practically unhinges his jaw and shoves a club triangle into his mouth.

"I'm surprised you didn't get pizza," Bex says. "That's the classic moving food."

He lifts a massive shoulder. "Eliza doesn't like pizza."

The hairs on the back of my neck prickle. I hate when he calls me pet names. But also—

"How do you know I don't like pizza?" I demand.

I mean, I don't. Red sauce is so not my thing. And it always gives me heartburn. I love pepperoni, though—on its own, or in a sandwich, or even on a salad.

Wyatt shrugs again. "You've mentioned it."

"No, I haven't." Because usually people make fun of me or tell me it's impossible that I don't like it. I just haven't had a good one. I haven't tried it enough. It's like sex. When it's good, it's good. When it's bad... it's still sex, so it can't be all bad. Right?

Sadly, just like pizza for me, sex has always been bad.

Including sex with this asshat.

Well—the actual time we were in bed was fine. Decent. Above average. It's just what happened afterward that's ruined my opinion.

"Sure, you have," he insists.

My eyes narrow. "When have we ever had pizza together?" I don't know why I'm pushing this. It's weird that he knows this about me when most people don't. Hell, I don't think Bex even realized I don't eat it. Usually, we order Thai or Mexican.

Past tense. Ordered. Because we won't be living together anymore.

Blowing out a breath, I pick at my sandwich, my appetite evaporating at the reminder. Even though I've moved criss-cross the country on multiple occasions, this one is hitting the hardest. I really liked my life in Boston. I have a good network of friends there, good friends. I have a job I loved.

Had.

Before things with Stephen got so tense it bled over into work, I really liked it there. I was the symphony's first fucking violin chair. I was tapped for major solos, and my music teaching gig was thriving.

And because my ex is an insecure asshole, now I have none of that.

Well, I'll still have my friends, even if now our friendship has to be nurtured from a distance.

Luckily, Austin wanted me. They even gave me a raise over what Boston was paying me, and with the lower cost of living, I'll finally be able to save a little. They liked me, just not enough to pay moving expenses, and even bootstrapping most of it myself, it hasn't been cheap. Plus, now I'll have to buy a car. I didn't need one back in Boston, but here in Texas, everything is driving distance.

Wyatt shakes his head, drawing my attention back to him. He always has to be the center of the fucking universe. His strawberry blond hair is a little longer than usual. There are red flecks in his light scruff. I bet if he grew it out, it would be red.

Why the fuck does he have to be so fucking hot? It's like the universe is taunting me, reminding me that the pretty people have everything and everyone else—the fat, the ugly, the boring—have nothing.

I have nothing.

"Fuck. I have to buy a car," I announce, and Bex winces.

"Have you figured out what car you want yet?" he asks.

"No. I figured I'd go to a used lot and find whatever's cheap and reliable."

If Mitch were here, he'd be able to talk the car salesperson into giving me a deal. As it is, shopping as a single woman, I'm sure they'll try to upsell and overcharge me on everything.

Wyatt makes a face. "Want me to go with you?"

I frown. "Why?"

He shrugs. "Moral support?"

"Seriously?" I laugh, and when he doesn't crack a smile, mine falls. "You're serious?"

"I have some free time tomorrow after I drop Bex at the airport."

"You'd do that for me?" I've never hidden my dislike of him, and even if he doesn't know why, he's never backed down from a fight.

And we fight. Constantly.

"You're my little sister's friend. Sure." He can't hide the distaste on his face, though.

"Don't act like I'm twisting your arm."

Bex looks between us. "This is perfect. You'll look out for her, won't you, Wy?"

He grunts.

"I don't need anyone to look out for me. I'm fine." Crossing my arms over my chest, I nearly knock over my Coke can.

Quick as lightning, Wyatt's hand darts out and stabilizes the can before it upends. He raises a brow, triumphant.

"Thanks," I mutter, rolling my eyes. So he has good reflexes. Whatever. He's a professional athlete. It's part of the job description.

"You'll invite her out, right?" Bex pushes. "I don't want her hiding away because she doesn't know anyone in town."

"I'll be fine. I've done this before," I remind her.

"Yeah, but it's different. With everything with you-know-who..."

My face pinches at the mention of my ex. "I won't be a hermit." Not any more than usual. I'm an introvert and a homebody by nature. "I've already got a lead on a bookclub and I'm sure I'll make friends at work. Besides, I have to get some teaching gigs lined up. I'll be too busy to go out much."

Bex laughs and pats my arm. "Yeah. Okay. Keep telling yourself that." She turns to her brother. "Make sure she doesn't bury herself in work, too."

Wyatt rolls his eyes. "She can take care of herself."

Yes! That's exactly what I've been saying.

Wait. I frown. Is he saying that because he doesn't want to help?

Not that I want him to help. I don't need it—from him, or from anyone else.

Bex glares at him.

"Fine," Wyatt sighs. "I'll invite her to hang out."

Great. Now he's talking about me like I'm not even here. I don't know what's worse, the infantilization or his ignoring my presence.

He throws his to-go container into a bag and reaches for mine. His eyebrows go up when he sees I haven't eaten my sandwich.

"Was tuna the wrong choice?"

I shake my head. "It's fine. I'm just not hungry, I guess."

Wyatt hums. "I'll put it in the fridge. You can eat it later."

That's... surprisingly thoughtful.

Damn it. Why does he have to be anything other than

the two-dimensional caricature of a villain I like to remember him as?

He deals with the trash, then lifts his toolbox.

"What do I need to build?"

###

Read more in Tripped Up, a best friend's brother, enemies to lovers romance.

MEET THE AUSTIN ACES

Austin Aces Hockey Club... where sworn enemies become lovers... on and off the ice.

Join eight of your favorite 🏒 romance authors and get in on the action...

One Touch by Linden Rowe
Unleashed by Jenna McCall
Power Play by C.M. Kane
Slapshot by TL Hamilton
Tripped Up by Allie Lasky
On Thin Ice by Rebecca Norinne Caudill
Puck Drop by Andie Bale
Goalie Interference by Kim Findlay

ALSO BY TL HAMILTON

M/F Sports Romance

The Perfect Stroke

Split - Kane & Darcy Pt 1

Shatter - Kane & Darcy Pt 2

Shock - Evie & Xavier

Fox Academy

Kicking it with the Winger Oscar & Mia

Austin Aces Hockey Club

Slapshot Cian & Blair

Warrior Sports League

False Start Weston & Gia

Wild Pitch Cami & Gage

∼

M/F Military Romantic Suspense

At All Costs

Target Me

Heal Me

∼

Contemporary RH

The One For Us

The not so secret life of a wish maker

Where in the world (Stand alone in 'The One For Us' universe)

Goldenfire Records

Not With the Band

Paranormal RH

Moon Dust Library/ Silver Springs Library Standalones

Moonlit Alexandrite

Moonlit Alexandrite: Crafty Seductions

Jewels Cafe: Jacinth

The Cursed Coven of Spells Hollow

Warrior Witch (co write with Katherine Isaac)

ABOUT THE AUTHOR

TL Hamilton hails from Melbourne, Australia, where she lives with her hubby, two (not so) little boys, and menagerie of animals.

The consummate daydreamer, TL writes all over the romance spectrum from romcom right through to the dark, gritty, hold onto your seats drama. Regardless of the story, you can guarantee you'll find relatable characters and steamy bedroom times between the covers of her books.

Reviews are the life blood of indie authors, so if you read her work and enjoy it, please consider leaving a review in exchange for her everlasting adoration.

Come and join the fun in her reader group on Facebook

www.tlhamiltonauthor.com

Acknowledgments

The lamp lights up and the final buzzer sounds on my second ice hockey romance!

I had so much fun writing Blair and Cian's story, and as always, I couldn't have done it without the love and support of my nearest and dearest.

First and foremost, I need to say a huge thank you to Mr H. From sending writing snacks to making sure our crazy house is quiet enough to write in, I would never get anything finished without you.

To my amazing Alpha reader, Jamie, I love you! From your invaluable feedback to your love of the characters, your demands for new words, and pointing out when my "Australian" is showing in the American dialogue, I couldn't do this without you.

To my editor, Zainab, I love you too, you crazy bitch. Your feedback never fails to light me up. You polish the hell out of my words and make them so shiny!

Thank you to Kristen Barrett at KB Barrett designs for the gorgeous cover, and Lonyaeli Graphics at Tantic Designs for the stunning interior graphics on the paperback.

I'd like to give a huge shout out to all the authors in the Austin Aces series, and say thank you for making this such a fun world to write in.

And while we're acknowledging authors (because they all deserve love and attention) I'd like to say a huge thank you to everyone in the community that I've had the honour of meeting.

The Victorian authors I get to see regularly — you guys inspire me. I love seeing what you're accomplishing and aspire to do as well as you all have.

And my author besties Katherine Isaac and Emmy Dee whose love languages are tiktok videos and memes: I love the shit out of you guys.

Finally, to you, the reader.

Whether this is your first book of mine, or you've been with me from the start (and let's face it, it's been a ride through a whole hell of a lot of different types of book) from the bottom of my heart THANK YOU for giving my work a chance, and I hope I'll see you again next time.

TL